RACE OF THE RADICAL

RACE
OF THE
RADICAL

by Fanny Howe

VIKING KESTREL

VIKING KESTREL
Viking Penguin Inc., 40 West 23rd Street, New York, New York 10010, U.S.A.
Penguin Books Ltd, Harmondsworth, Middlesex, England
Penguin Books Australia Ltd, Ringwood, Victoria, Australia
Penguin Books Canada Limited, 2801 John Street, Markham, Ontario, Canada L3R 1B4
Penguin Books (N.Z.) Ltd, 182–190 Wairau Road, Auckland 10, New Zealand

First published in 1985 by Viking Penguin Inc.
Published simultaneously in Canada

Printed in the United States of America by
R. R. Donnelley & Sons Company, Crawfordsville, Indiana
Set in Times Roman.
1 2 3 4 5 89 88 87 86 85

Library of Congress Cataloging in Publication Data
Howe, Fanny.   Race of the radical.
Summary: Twelve-year-old Alex Porter, an expert racer on a lighter-than-air bicycle,
fights to save his bike from irresponsible race promoters.
    [1. Bicycle racing—Fiction] I. Title.
PZ7.H83725Rac 1985   [Fic]   85-40445   ISBN 0-670-80557-2

To Jessica and J.J.

RACE OF THE RADICAL

1

Alex was awakened by the sound of his mother in the pickup truck. He could tell by her loud mouth that she was out under the hood, working on the carburetor. She always sang country-western, while under the hood. He climbed out of bed and twisted open the venetian blinds. She was in under the hood all right, while Robinson and Rosie were riding their bikes in circles around the truck. Alex stretched, yawned, and flashed on the fear that he was late for school.

No! It was the end of June, summer vacation, and it wasn't even a weekday. He grinned to himself. The foothills would stay pretty clear of smog because it was Saturday—a big day at the BMX race track in nearby Meridian. He would be able to see the clear brown lines of the foothills all day and into the evening when the shadows got deep.

Alex slipped on some jeans and a T-shirt and aimed for the kitchen. The house was a single-level ranch. The three kids had rooms in one area, the parents in another, and they were separated from each other by a living room, dinette, and kitchen. Out beyond the patio in back there was a pool, and out beyond the pool there was the little metal shed where Alex's father invented things.

Alex, at twelve, had his mother's black hair and blue eyes. He was of average height, slender and muscular from lifting weights and riding his bike. His brother and sister both looked like their father, who was blond and fair-skinned. Robinson, age five, was very plump, though, with a pair of squishy cheeks and full, pink lips. Rosie, who was six, was slim and dainty and pale with white blond hair. Her Barbie dolls lay all over the house, under tables and chairs, and by toilets. You would see a shapely leg or arm sticking out of the strangest places, or a whole doll body with wild hair, sprawled in the chair you were just about to sit on.

Looking out the kitchen window, Alex saw one of them floating in the pool, as if drowned. He could see it through the enormous tropical plants his mother kept on the patio. The doll floating there didn't move an inch, showing that the pump was off.

Alex went out to turn it back on, so the pool would stay clean for the day, and saw his father in the shed. He

4

also was on vacation. Now he was surrounded by all kinds of tools and parts, but Alex didn't go see what he was working on. For several months his father had promised him "a bike that will practically fly," and he had caught glimpses of spokes, cranks, tires, and even handlebars through the door. But he didn't peek. His father was a perfectionist, and Alex believed he would never finish the bike because he would never be satisfied. That was frustrating. So Alex contined to ride his GT, adding and repairing parts as if he would have that same frame forever.

Alex turned on the pump and the doll began to slowly twirl around on the surface of the pool. He watched it, daydreaming about the race that day. Two of his heroes—pros who had raced since they were his age—would be there, competing with each other for the first time. He couldn't even decide which one he hoped would win, he liked them both so much. He planned to get their autographs, and to race the best he could and maybe catch their attention. Alex's total obsession was BMX.

His mother, Mariel, was an announcer at the races. She wasn't like the other mothers in that college town in southern California. She wasn't into jogging, or health food, or taking classes. She smoked, drank whiskey, ate junk food, and drove a pickup truck around town. She repaired cars for people at home, so she could take care of Robinson and Rosie. Alex's father, Mr. Porter, was her exact opposite. He was from the east coast, an aerospace engineer who played the violin with professors and invented a portable fountain that was beginning to sell. He didn't smoke and didn't know anything about cars. Alex didn't realize what a strange couple they made until his friends began to say so. All Alex's friends liked his mother.

He went into the house to grab some breakfast before those same friends arrived to go to the race. He ate half a box of Frosted Flakes in a mixing bowl placed on his knee. With his free hand he held a joystick and played Donkey Kong Junior on the Coleco set. He was feeling good when Robinson came crashing into the living room and demanded a turn with the joystick.

"Go away, Robinson! Can't you see I'm busy?" Alex snapped.

The little boy's lower lip shot out, his chin stiffened and his eyes grew wet.

"Tsch. What a baby," Alex muttered, but he gave Robinson the joystick anyway. He hated to make him cry, it was so easy.

Robinson smiled and poked once at the controls, then looked out the window at the pool, bored.

Alex let out a huge sigh and grabbed back the joystick. It always happened that way. "No peace," he said to himself. He poured the leftover milk in the bowl down his throat.

Sometimes he wished he could go to a desert island for a week, just with his bike and maybe his best friend Rennie. Little kids could drive him crazy, especially when he babysat. Rosie wasn't too bad, but Robinson could drive a person to drink, as his mother would say. He turned off the Coleco.

And now his house was about to be invaded by four boys from the neighborhood. They were decent racers, and were just as excited as he was about the pros coming to the track that day. But he really felt like being alone. Or on the road. Sometimes he and his mother traveled hundreds of miles to race. He loved that. They would play the radio and stare out the window at the mountains and the sea, the palm trees and flowers and little Spanish houses, the orange and lemon groves. They'd go to wineries and to Mexican restaurants and camp outside the tracks with other travelers and talk BMX until they all fell asleep.

"Wake up," said Robinson, trying to snap his fingers in front of Alex's eyes. There was no snap though.

"Okay, okay, let's go outside."

"Mommy says get dressed for the race!" Rosie called, and she ran by on her way to her room.

Robinson followed, all smiles, because it was time for him to put on his helmet.

By nine-thirty that morning, there were four other boys sitting beside Alex in front of the house. They were all dressed to race, in different colored pants and shirts, with padded shoulders, legs and arms, and helmets. Two of the boys had a number 1 on their shirt backs, one had a 4, another a 12; Alex had a 7.

They were waiting for Rosie and Robinson to come out in their uniforms and get going to the track. The back of the truck was stacked with shiny chrome bikes and Mariel was sitting in front with the engine running, a cigarette dangling out of her mouth and the radio blasting deep funk. Finally Robinson waddled out the door in his red racing suit, a helmet hiding his whole face, except for his smile. Rosie followed and got in front with her mother. All the boys piled into the back, pulling up Robinson.

"I'm number 1!" he announced, and his voice echoed inside the helmet. "See?" He wiggled around to show his back. "I'm going to win."

Everyone said, "Wow, that's great," and tried not to laugh. Robinson always thought he was a genius, and never seemed to notice when he was the only five-year-old racing in a class by himself.

All the way over to the track, the boys talked about Mark and Pat, the two pros, making bets on which one would come in first. Alex had seen them each race separately, but never against each other. They were members of the same League, but were sponsored by two different bike companies. Alex, who longed to get a sponsor himself, prayed that he would do his best that day and get the most out of his old GT. And then, maybe, he could travel to races alone, without his family. . . .

The track was already teeming with activity when they got there and unloaded the bikes. Robinson rode off immediately, wobbling under the weight of his helmet. He was riding a small, fat-wheeled Mongoose, and Rosie followed him on her Red Line, with her pale hair sticking out from under her helmet.

"I'll be up in the stands," Mariel told Alex. "You take care of the kids, honey . . . and good luck!"

She gave him a kiss and disappeared into the crowd with her Jackson Five thermos full of coffee.

The track was considered one of the best in the country,

since a lot of work had been done on it this spring. What used to be pretty rough and untended was now well groomed and smooth. Trees had been cut, so the track was both wider and longer, with the starting hill twelve feet high. The first jump was a tabletop; then came a wide berm, curving like the hollowed-out wall of a tunnel, leading into a six-foot drop. Then there was a six-foot drop and stepdrop jump, a roller-coaster berm, and four whoop-de-dos: plenty to make you pay attention when you were riding at high speed, crammed between five or six other racers in your group, or "moto."

There were several campers parked beside the track, and folding chairs were set up around them, near big coolers stuffed with food and big tool kits stuffed with bicycle repair equipment. There was a small concession stand where you could buy a numberplate for the day, and some junk food. Alex registered himself, Robinson, and Rosie, all the time looking around for the two pros. He could tell which campers were theirs by all the decals plastered on bumpers. But the crowd was larger than usual— over a hundred registered racers—and he couldn't see them anywhere.

By ten the sun was hot and the foothills were slightly hazy from leftover smog mixed with heat waves. The racing began promptly. Alex's mother was the announcer, shouting down through the speaker over the tinny music:

"Go for it, Yellow Submarine, grab the fourth! . . . There goes Stu nabbing a killer holeshot—bang! He got his first— and look at Joey Ricardo pass T. J. in the Spiderman suit—"

Alex wandered around, pushing his bike, and finally he spotted his two heroes surrounded by fans getting their autographs. He hesitated and decided not to look stupid like that and to forget about their autographs. He was surprised by how normal they looked in the flesh that day—sort of pimply and short. The kids who surrounded them were all embarrassed and red-faced, as if the pros were gods visiting from space. Alex looked at them critically, but not at their bikes.

Alex had always loved his bike, but not this day. In comparison with the pros' bikes, it looked pathetic. The handlebars were scratched and there was a hairline crack in the crossbar he hoped no one would see. He wanted, so badly, to do well, he found himself feeling more nervous than usual. Now it was Rosie's moto, though, and he hurried over to cheer her on. She was racing against four other girls, but she got off to a great start and stayed in the lead all the way.

It was time for him to get in line for his moto. He was third in line with the group. His hands were sweating inside his gloves as his mother yelled:

"Uh-oh, Billy took a spill, looks like Greg annihilated him and Paul in one fell swoop . . . But look who's taking advantage of the mess! It's Sammy Brentano taking that berm like it was a runway, and there he goes, passing Brian and Greg—and—uh-oh—down goes Sammy—bites the dust. . . . Greg's dangerous today!"

Alex looked back and saw that the pros were only three motos behind him, which meant they would probably see him race. He just wanted to get it over with now, but there was a break because Billy was still lying on his back in the track, injured. Alex could see two men coming out of the crowd to check on him, and then Rennie came out too. It made Alex smile to see him. He knew he was missing something, or someone that day. It was Rennie!

He wasn't wearing his Diamondback outfit, which meant he wasn't going to race. Again. Rennie was sixteen and could have become a pro that summer—everyone said so—except he couldn't afford to race. His bike needed new parts, but his father had been laid off from work and was sick, so Rennie had to earn money to bring home. He never complained about it; that was the weird thing. Rennie was Mexican, dark-haired with honey-colored skin, and though he didn't go to school much, he was really smart. He dropped in at school about twice a week and got good grades. The rest of the time he fished, picked fruit in the orchards, or just roamed around alone. Alex's mother paid him to help her with her auto-repair business, and though she always asked him to stay for dinner or for the night with Alex, he wouldn't. He carried a sleeping bag around and slept outside a lot, as if he didn't live anywhere. That was just the way he wanted it to be.

He and Alex were unlikely friends, as Alex's father would say; but for some reason they really liked being together.

Now it was Alex's turn to race and he concentrated on the brown, dusty track dropping down ahead of him. The other 12-experts, eight in all, pressed their front tires against the gate as Alex's mother said, "Here they come—the wildest bunch of mega-major-superterrific complete and

11

total winners you ever saw . . ." Alex clenched his teeth, squeezed his handlebars, and glanced back at the pros to see if they were watching.

The gate slammed down and he got off to a poor start. He was jammed between three bikes after the first berm, and he knew he wouldn't even come in fourth. With his eyes burning, he pedaled as hard as he could, but finally the only way he could save his pride was to show off. So he lagged behind all the other racers, as if he had planned it this way, and on the stepdrop jump he did a sidehack that turned into a brilliant tabletop at the end. Everyone shouted and clapped. He picked up speed after the roller-coaster berm and scaled all four whoop-de-dos, cruised toward one last bump at the finish, climbed into a wheelie, and fell flat on his side, the pedal jumping into his ankle. He felt dust all over the side of his face and heard the crowds laughing.

He got up fast and rode into the crowd, jerking off his helmet and spitting dirt out of his mouth. Robinson ran up to him, followed by Rosie.

"You were really good!" cried Robinson.

Alex counted to ten. He felt awful, he had made such a fool of himself. He was mad at his bike and his mother and blamed them both for everything.

Rosie said, "Your start was stinky, Alex. You better practice more."

"Thanks for telling me."

He pushed by her to where he saw Rennie sitting on a tree stump with a can of Coke. He was grinning.

"Don't say anything," said Alex with a half smile, "I know I blew it."

"Really? Maybe you should take up trick riding in a skate park. Here, Robinson, have a bite," said Rennie as he held out a Twix bar.

"Did you see me win?" asked Rosie. Like most girls, she had a crush on Rennie and went to sit beside him.

"You looked beautiful," said Rennie, "a lot better than your brother."

"It's my mother's fault," said Alex. "Why can't she just be normal and stay home and be quiet? She makes me nervous."

"She never did before," said Rennie. "Maybe it's your bike, man, maybe that's the problem. After all, a GT . . . ?"

"Hey, you know a GT is what you want. Don't talk it down," said Alex.

"It's not his bike,' said Rosie, "it's his starts. He needs to practice. Right, Rennie?" And she looked up at him as if he was a movie star.

The other announcer took over for Alex's mother, saying, "My turn. This little lady needs a break, especially now that her old man has stopped being a mad scientist for a little while and has decided to join us plain folks over here. . . ." Lots of laughs from the crowd. "Our pro class is coming up in a minute. . . . Fasten your safety belts."

"I wonder why Dad's here," said Alex.

"I'll go find him," said Rosie, and off she rode, with Robinson following as usual.

"I better hose down the dust," said Rennie, who kept the track groomed at the races he wasn't in. He walked away, while Alex went back to the trackside to get a good view of his heroes racing. There were only four pros racing, and Pat and Mark were in the middle, side by side, when the gate fell. Alex watched them closely, figuring out their moves and admiring the way they took the berms and jumps. Pat and Mark raced neck and neck all the way to the roller-coaster berm, when Mark moved into the lead. The crowd was going crazy, and Alex's head was pounding, his throat ached and he felt like he wanted to cry. Watching the pros do so well made him hate himself. If only he could blame Robinson!

"It's your bike," he heard his father say.

"I can't blame it on my bike!" he replied, and swung around. His father was right behind him, holding a bike Alex never saw before. Not that one bike and not any one like it. Its parts were like thin shiny tubes, and it was sparkling silver in the sunlight.

"What's that?" Alex asked, touching the seat.

"It's the bike I promised you. It's fiberglass. Pick it up."

Alex did as he was told, but he felt that he was in a dream, or in shock. He lifted the bike from the crossbar and it floated up through the air, as if it were made of paper.

"Fiberglass?" he said.

"Well, fiberglass and chrome-moly. I figured we needed to make the most lightweight bike in the world. And this is it. It's not perfect. But I figured you might as well try it and we'll fix up any problems as they develop. I'm not satisfied with the crankshaft. That could weigh less."

"Wow, Dad. Thanks!" Alex said, and leaned his old GT against his father, as if he were a tree. Then he hopped

14

on the new bike and began to ride it through the crowd toward the parking lot. Behind him he heard the announcer shouting about what a great race it was. Pat had pulled into first, ahead of Mark, at the last minute. But Alex didn't care. He just wanted to test-ride this bike, which shone so brightly he could hardly look at it.

His sense of disappointment and tension disappeared as he pedaled across the dusty lot. He picked up speed, little by little, and turned out onto the road heading toward the foothills. The wheels spun faster and faster until it seemed there were no wheels at all, and no ground either. He did a wheelie over a jump by a ditch and found himself soaring several feet off the ground. His heart leaped up. He felt he was flying!

Alex turned the bike around and raced back to the track, smiling all the way. He had to show everyone!

2

"Come on, you guys. It's flying time!" Alex could hear his mother, back at the bullhorn, announcing a beginner's race for boys ages six and under. Only two were registered: Robinson and a boy called his "emeny." They were riding twin Mongooses, side by side, and with a lot of effort over the berms. Alex's mother called out with a laugh, "Let's chew the dust!"

This gave Robinson a charge and he pedaled hard, wobbling up the hill, which suddenly looked very high. He got the lead on his "emeny." The crowds were laughing and shouting encouragement at the two little boys under their enormous helmets. Then Robinson made the mistake of looking back to see where the other boy was. He was at the top of a hill and promptly started rolling backward.

"Don't you know," shouted his mother, "you're never supposed to look back!"

The other boy churned past Robinson, rolled down the hill, and bumped over the whoop-de-dos, finally coming in first. Robinson followed, as red as a beet. He threw his bike down at his big brother's feet and stamped into the crowds, looking for his father.

"Rennie!" Alex shouted.

Alex placed himself on his bike, as if he were modeling it for a magazine, and stood with the handlebars gleaming in the sun, while Rennie came up to see him.

"What are you grinning about?" asked Rennie. Then he saw the bike. He crouched down to look at it more closely, his eyes wide and shining.

"Wow, man, is this the one your dad made for you? Wow, wow! Can I pick it up? Get off a minute."

Alex handed the bike over and watched Rennie lift it with his right hand high over his head. "It must weigh about two pounds," he sighed. "Oh, man. I can't wait to see you ride this."

"Go on. You try it," said Alex.

"Can I?"

"Sure. Go on down the road. I have plenty of time before my moto's called again."

Rennie set off on the bike, and someone stepped up behind Alex and put a hand on his shoulder. Alex swung around. It was Rick, a junior in the high school, and an expert BMX racer. He was wearing a Schwinn T-shirt with his name sewed on the back in red. Rick was, as usual, flanked by his two friends, Jeff and Stu. All three were blond, with blue eyes and square jaws. They looked like beach bums, with their year-round tans and dark glasses. Everyone knew they were rich and each had a great bike, even though none of them was completely obsessed by BMX.

"Your friend's riding an awesome bike," he said to Alex.

"You're not kidding."

"Speedy Gonzales, right? We should make him a special label for his dirty T-shirt."

They all smiled in a bored sort of way, and wandered off to a pickup truck. They soon drove away, as if saying to everyone there that the race—a local—wasn't worth their time. Alex watched them go and sighed to himself. While those three were reasonably nice to him, they were mean to Rennie and always had been. Their crowd didn't, as a rule, get close to Mexican students in the high school. But Rennie was their special target, because girls found him "gorgeous" and "romantic." His loner ways made him special around the high school, and the boys, like Rick, were envious of Rennie's freedom.

Alex watched Rennie returning, full speed, on the bike. His black hair blew back from his smooth forehead and he wore a big smile on his face.

"Oh, man! It's like flying," he called.

"Let's go tell my dad."

Rennie pushed the new bike and Alex rolled along on Robinson's fat little Mongoose until they came to where

Alex's father was leaning over fixing some boy's handlebars with a wrench. Robinson got all excited about the new bike and forgot about being mad.

"It's almost time for you to ride again, Alex. Hurry!" he cried.

"This bike is phenomenal," Rennie told Mr. Porter. "You could make a million dollars off it."

"Hmm," mused Alex's father, "I guess I could. Almost. But I'm not satisfied with the gooseneck or the crankshaft. It's not quite right. See?"

He showed Rennie the large piece of metal holding the handlebars onto the frame and said, "This should be much less conspicuous, and lighter too."

"I don't know how it could be much lighter," said Rennie. "I personally never rode such a featherweight machine. Can't wait to see Alex fly around the track."

And fly he did—through the second and the third races, coming in first both times. His father, who rarely attended these events, was beaming and shouting, just like the other fathers. Alex felt so lucky he could hardly stand it. The bike was the center of attention, and so was he. But only he knew what it felt like to approach a roller-coaster berm and skim across the dust, as if he was an inch off the ground. And only he knew how it felt to fly over the crest of the hill and see the ground far below him. His mother was shouting, "Boy, that bike can fly. It has wings! Watch him head for the clouds, guys!" And he heard the applause and shouts as if he really was heading for the blue sky, with the silver tubes shining between his hands like thin bands of water.

20

After the third race the pros came over to where Alex stood with his bike, waiting at the trophy stand. Alex suddenly felt as if he was doing a television commercial for himself and his new bike. He answered all their questions about the fiberglass, the chrome-moly, the shape of the handlebars, as if he himself had made the bike what it was. Mark and Pat were obviously impressed, even envious; but they were generous in their praise, too, and encouraging.

"You should think of going pro with this bike," Mark said. "I bet you could get some factory to sponsor you."

"Seriously," Pat agreed, "I bet a magazine would want to run a feature on the Radical too. You should look into that."

"Yeah, I guess maybe I will," Alex said, "after I get used to it, that is."

"Boy, feel how light it is!" Mark exclaimed, and lifted the Radical high up and handed it to Pat. "Featherweight!"

Alex watched them and remembered the many times he had examined their faces and uniforms and bikes in magazines himself. He couldn't believe they were right in front of him, treating him as an equal. And he couldn't help thinking that maybe they were right. He should go pro.

They told him to take care of the bike and left. Alex went back to his father.

"Dad, it's beautiful," he announced, and actually rolled Robinson around on it a few times.

That day Alex got a first. It was a tall blue trophy with a silver bike on top. After the awards presentation, his family headed home with dusty but happy faces. Rennie came along, and even though they planned a full barbecue, he insisted that they drop him at the Taco Bell near their house.

"You're weird," said Rosie. "Don't you ever eat anything except enchiladas?"

"Yeah, burritos," he said, and winked at her.

"But they're always from Taco Bell."

"Only my sister makes them that good," he said.

"I only eat hamburger," Robinson announced, "and apples."

"It's true," his father laughed. "He only eats hamburger—well done."

"And Captain Crunch," Rosie put in.

"And chips, any kind," added Alex.

"And chocolate," Robinson admitted.

"But Rennie only eats enchiladas and burritos from Taco Bell," said Mr. Porter with a smile.

"Bring them back and eat them by the pool," Alex told Rennie. "My mom expects you."

Mariel followed in the truck with all the bikes, and beeped loudly when they dropped Rennie by the side of the road. She knew his habits as well as those of her own children. He was carrying his backpack and sleeping bag, and would probably have a shower and a swim at their house before roaming away on his own. He lived about two miles down the main street, near the freeway, in a row of tiny pastel-colored adobe houses. There were cactus plants in his front yard, and a small vegetable garden that his father tended. The house contained two bedrooms, and there were four children besides Rennie. Every day he checked in there and sometimes he stayed, but generally, when the weather allowed it, he preferred to lie out under the stars in a special place of his own. In a corner of a small state park on the edge of town was a clearing in a grove of eucalyptus trees where he could lie in the quiet of the night and see the stars. Only Alex knew about this place, and he envied Rennie for having the courage to be such a loner.

"I wish I could be like Rennie," said Robinson with a big pout. "I'd even eat burritos . . . without cheese, or beans. Just hamburger."

"Why do you wish you were like him?" asked his father.

"Because everyone does."

"I wonder why."

"Because he's so free," said Robinson as solemnly as if they were discussing the state of the nation.

"Hmm. I guess you could say that. But aren't you glad you have your family?"

"No," said Robinson matter-of-factly. "I'm glad I have a pool."

They all groaned as they drove into the garage.

Within fifteen minutes, everyone was in the pool, cooling off from the heat and dust of the track. Then Mariel Porter started the briquettes heating up for the barbecue, and Rennie came in to shower and swim. Mr. Porter fussed over the new bike, readjusting parts and even suggested stripping it down and starting all over again.

"No, Dad, please leave it," Alex begged. "Tomorrow there's a State National I want to race in. . . . Come on. It's fine."

"But it might not pass inspection," his father said. "Don't they inspect them before every race?"

"Of course they do, and of course it will," said Mariel, throwing chicken onto the grille, so smoke shot up around her. "Just leave it alone."

"What will you call it?" asked Rosie.

"Good question," said Mr. Porter. "We'll have to think of a name."

"I have to name my goldfish too!" cried Robinson, and he ran off to his room.

Each person had a bunch of suggestions for a name for the bike, ranging from serious names like Silver Streak to silly names like Monkey Shine. Meanwhile Robinson set his goldfish bowl beside the pool and christened his lonely fish Prince, after the singer. "That's rad," said Rennie, swimming to the edge of the pool. "I like that name for a fish."

"Rad?" asked Mr. Porter, puzzled.

"Short for radical," said Alex, and then his eyes lit up. "That's it!"

"What?"

"We'll call the bike the Radical . . . it's perfect!"

"Hey, great, man. I like it," Rennie called approvingly.

Everyone agreed, except Rosie who still liked Monkey Shine. Alex took the bike away from his father and wheeled it to the edge of the pool. Its reflection glittered like silver mica across the shimmering blue water.

"Want me to smash a beer bottle on it?" called his mother. "That's how they usually do it."

"Thanks, but no thanks, Mom. I think I'll just splash a little water on it," Alex replied with a smile, and he leaned down and flicked water onto the crossbar. "I hereby dub you the Radical," he announced.

Then Robinson stuck his chubby fingers in his goldfish bowl and extracted the fish.

"Da-dah! I hereby call you Prince," he announced, and the goldfish shot between his fingers, into the air, and landed with a tiny plop in the water. Everyone stared in disbelief as the fish cheerfully swam away. Rennie then dove for it, Mr. Porter ran to get the net on the long pole and the others shouted instructions.

Suddenly, the goldfish disappeared. Rennie climbed out of the water, and everybody watched while the pool grew still and clear, while above them the sun was turning as gold as the fish itself. There was nothing there. The fish was gone. Everyone but Robinson knew it had gone into one of the drains.

"I'll get you another one," Mariel told Robinson. "Don't cry."

"But where is it?" the little boy kept asking, mystified. "Where did it go?"

"It's a mystery . . . a complete mystery," Alex murmured, staring into the still water as though he had no idea.

This time would not be the last that he murmured these words to himself.

3

Alex had registered the Radical by nine-thirty the next morning. He knew the track at Azusa well. He had raced there several times before and wasn't expecting any surprises. His mother was not going to referee, but the other parents running this race were friends of hers and she decided to stay and watch.

"Good. That means I don't have to watch Robinson," Alex thought, and scanned the crowds for Rennie.

It was a hot morning. People had set themselves up around their campers and on beach chairs, using every available shadow. They even brought their own shade, in the form of umbrellas and big hats. Kids were practicing on the track, and dust flew up in all directions. The brown foothills, against a smoggy blue sky, ringed the valley and made the track all the hotter and dustier.

Alex left his bike with his mother and walked around, checking the crowds. He saw Rick, Jeff, and Stu, and they saw him.

"Hey, Alex, why aren't you with Geronimo?"

He knew they meant Rennie. "I don't know," he said. "Have you seen him?"

"Yeah, somewhere over there," said Rick in an angry voice. "You just tell him to keep away from any and all girls. Okay?"

"I can't tell him what to do," Alex told him.

"Give it a try," said Stu, stepping forward. "And if he doesn't listen, tell him we're paying attention."

"What are you doing," Alex asked, "pretending to be hoods or something?"

He walked away from them, trying to look as if he thought they were extremely childish. Actually, he was a little nervous. Stu was the son of a minister, but he was known to be really wicked. It was sort of a joke that Reverend Taylor's son was the worst behaved boy in town. He didn't just limit himself to playing pranks, either. He did do really vicious things, like slashing tires, or knocking a biker clear off the track in the middle of a race, or drag-racing girls on the freeways. That was dangerous.

Alex found Rennie beside the benches, where people were all lined up in the full sun. Their eyes were all squinty. Again Rennie was not wearing his racing uniform.

"Why not?" Alex asked him.

"I can't afford it. I don't care. It's too hot."

Rennie was working on tightening the seat on a small boy's bike. Alex told him what Rick and Stu had said.

"I'm not going to do anything just to please them," he responded, and bounced the palms of his hands down on the bike seat to test it. "There. That should do it."

He waved to a girl his age. Addie Sparks was her name, and she came over in a kind of punk outfit made up of a silver miniskirt and a pink harness-top shirt with sequins. Her long, copper-brown hair was shining in the sun, and she smiled sweetly at Rennie. Alex looked at Rick and his friends on the other side of the track. They were looking at Rennie.

"Thanks, Ren," said Addie. "I'll tell my brother to win. For you."

"Okay. I'll be watching," Rennie replied with a smile.

He watched her walk away, and it was obvious to Alex that they liked each other.

"Jeff and Stu and Rick are going to kill you, Rennie. That's Rick's old girlfriend."

"As long as it's all over between them, what do I care? She's nice, isn't she?"

"Yeah."

"And really pretty too."

Alex shrugged. "Not my type," he told Rennie, even though he didn't think much about girls.

The annnouncer started shouting about everyone finding out their moto number and getting in line. Some canned music was turned on, and kids crowded around the posted lists looking for their names and race numbers. Alex was

29

in the sixteenth moto. He was racing against some really top 12-experts, six in all. He had time to kill before his race, which was disappointing. He felt he could hardly wait to get out on the track with the Radical.

"Robinson's in number six moto," said Rennie. "You better tell him to line up. He's actually competing against four other kids. . . . One of them is Addie's little brother, Moses."

"Wow," said Alex, making a face. "Big deal."

They walked over to where Mariel Porter was seated with a Coke and cigarette, talking to some friends of hers. All the parents were wearing shorts and T-shirts, the day was so hot.

"Alex, you babysit your bike now. It's making me nervous," she said.

The Radical leaned beside her, shining like sterling, from its spokes to the handlebars.

"Can I ride around on it?" Rennie asked.

"Sure."

"Alex, you take Robinson over to his moto," his mother instructed him.

Alex twisted his mouth and sighed in irritation. Sometimes Robinson drove him crazy, and embarrassed him with the stupid things he said.

"I'm going to lose," the little boy told Alex now.

"No, you aren't. Come on."

"Why not?"

"Because I said so."

"Am I good at it?" Robinson asked Alex, and his voice almost echoed inside his helmet, while the strap covered his whole chin.

"What do you think?"

"No," said Robinson. "I'm not good at it. You are."

"Oh, be quiet," Alex said, and pushed him into line beside the other five-year-olds. "Just do your best, and this time don't look back!"

Then everyone stood still while the tinny tape played the national anthem. There was no wind to blow the two flags—one the state flag, the other American—up on the stands. The heat beat down on everyone's faces, although it was only noon. Across the squinting faces, Alex saw Rennie. He was standing with Addie Sparks, and they were not paying attention to the song, but were admiring the Radical. Rick, Jeff, and Stu were watching them leaning over the bike together, and they looked mad.

The gate banged down, and the first moto was off and pedaling. The voice in the bullhorn was shouting excitedly. Alex waited to see Robinson bike his first race, before going to retrieve the Radical. He stood at the finish line, waiting to cheer his little brother on. Robinson was at the gate with four other boys and two fathers. They were readying their sons for the big race. Alex's mother came and joined him at the finish line.

"Boy, I hate fathers like that," she muttered. "They get so involved in their child's success, it's disgusting."

The gate slammed down, and Robinson was off to a good start, while the two fathers stood roaring orders, their faces bright red.

Mariel began to scream: "Come on, Robby honey! Pump those pedals. . . . Stay close to the side. . . . Don't stop to cruise!"

Alex nudged her. "Be quiet, Mom. I thought you couldn't stand parents who got so involved."

"It's different for me," she retorted.

And they both began shouting as Robinson rolled along the edge of the berm, ahead of the other three, his back bent over and his short legs pedaling hard, as if his wheels were millstones.

"Little Mister Porter has the lead there. . . . Look at that tyke roll!" the announcer shouted.

Robinson climbed up to the crest of the hill, wobbled, and then rolled down it, grinning under his helmet. Alex and his mother were jumping up and down when he came in number one. He couldn't comment because the strap was in his mouth.

"Here go the Powder Puffs!" the announcer called, as the 15-novice girls' moto started off down the track.

Mariel winced. "I've got to tell him to stop calling the girls such stupid names," she said, and marched off to do just that.

"Oh, Mom," Alex groaned under his breath. Sometimes she embarrassed him as much as Robinson did.

Then Rennie wheeled the Radical up beside him and Addie sighed, saying how beautiful it was.

"I could beat those girls in a race any time," Robinson said, and spat the strap out of his mouth.

They all watched the fifteen-year-olds move slowly around the track, and heard the announcer laugh and say, "Those girls ride like they're out for a Sunday cruise."

Robinson agreed, and so did Rennie and Addie. But Alex didn't say anything, because he was watching Rick look at Rennie as if he could kill him. "He still likes Addie," Alex thought. "Rennie better watch out."

By the time Alex's moto was called, almost everyone was off eating lunch. Not even Rennie watched while he sped into first place, lifting his bike slightly up in the front so it flew over all six whoop-de-dos. Even the announcer didn't pay much attention. Everyone was really hot, grumpy, and tired.

The morning wore into the afternoon, with lots of grownups leaving early to go home and get cool, while only the determined bikers stayed. Twice Alex took the Radical off for a ride on a shady road along the foothills, where he could feel a cool breeze. He couldn't ride the bike enough. It was like being awake and dreaming at the same time. The bike seemed half alive, and he could imagine what it must have been like to have a horse you could ride everywhere. He felt as if the bike was his friend, and he would never be alone as long as he was with it.

During his third race, Rennie got a lift to Taco Bell with Addie, who worked at the counter there. So no one was there to cheer for Alex when he came in first. The announcer this time mentioned his bike, though, and a crowd of kids came over to look at it and touch it.

Finally Rennie returned with a burrito for Alex and said, "Rick and those creeps are down at Taco Bell right now. They made these threats—oh, well."

He looked worried and stared off into space. Alex begged him to say what they threatened.

"Never mind. I just don't want to mess with them," Rennie said. "Rick's father is my father's doctor."

"Well, then leave Addie alone."

"No, and anyway try and tell *her* that."

"Here. Take the Radical and go for a ride. It will make you feel a lot better. I guarantee," said Alex, imitating a salesman.

Rennie happily took the bike and aimed for that shady road bordering the foothills. Alex admired the trophies while the last races continued. His would be a beautiful sea-green one today, a new color to add to his collection, which ranged from pink to navy blue, passing through every color in the rainbow. Almost. Now he imagined this one, seated on the shelf in his bedroom, tall and shining.

"You're doing good, kid," a man said to him then, interrupting his thoughts. "You can be proud of yourself."

"Thanks," said Alex, looking up at him.

He was a heavyset man in a gray nylon shirt. He didn't look familiar, and Alex knew almost every face from some other race at that track. This man looked rich, even though he was sweating. Pressed khaki pants, black loafers, a gold watch and a gold chain made him look out of place on the hot, dusty track. His eyes were blue in a thick beef-red face.

"You going to be racing next week?" he asked Alex.

"I guess," Alex said. "It's the biggest race before the State National."

"Yeah, I know. I'll be there too. I'm from a factory. I sponsor some of these kids."

"What factory?" asked Alex with curiosity. He had never

34

actually met one of the people who sponsored professional BMXers.

"Rainbow Toys. . . . I never saw a bike like yours."

"I know," said Alex proudly. "It's called the Radical."

"You don't say. The Radical . . . Where did you get it?"

"My dad," Alex told him.

And then he didn't say any more because he saw his mother approaching with a don't-talk-to-strangers look on her face.

"Hi, Mom!" he called quickly.

"See you next week," the man muttered, and tapped Alex's shoulder in a chummy way.

Alex watched him walk away from the table laden with bright-colored trophies and disappear into some parked trucks and campers. His mother came up beside him. "Who was that man you were talking to?" she asked.

"A sponsor."

"Did he ask you—?"

"No, Mom. I think he was really interested in the Radical and not in me."

"Oh, I see," she said vaguely, then added, "I'm really interested in Robinson and not in that man. Where is he?"

"I don't know. Somewhere."

"You're supposed to keep an eye on him, Alex," Mariel scolded. "You have no idea how dangerous this world is. Kids are being kidnapped by the hour. Now you go find him and bring him here. They're about to announce the winners."

Alex walked off angrily. He had heard his mother's

kidnapping speech too many times already, and deep down he didn't believe a word of it. Still, he was glad to see his brother's blond head bobbing among a tangle of bikes. He didn't want to ruin a great day by getting in trouble.

"Come on, Rob," he called. "Mom wants you. And I think you'll be getting a first."

"I know I'm getting a first," said Robinson in his Big Man voice, as Alex called it. "I won all the races, dummy."

"Okay then. Come on," Alex said impatiently. "And next time don't go wandering off."

Together they returned to the table and found a gathering collection of winners, eager to be announced. The crush of bikes and kids, of sweat and heat, made everyone impatient.

Mariel said, "I'll wait for you guys in the car."

"No, Mommy!" screeched Robinson. "I want you to see me win."

"Good. That means I can leave," said Alex, and went to join some friends.

His mother stayed then, and after a few minutes, Rennie arrived on foot and leaned down over the sheets of papers listing the winners.

"I better see how Moses did," he said.

"You like him better than me," Robinson muttered with a pout.

Rennie laughed. "No, I don't. I just want to see."

"Well, you can't," Robinson told him and covered the papers with his dirty little hand.

"Alex!" Rennie called. "Your brother is being a brat."

Alex was out of earshot, talking to some kids, and just shrugged and made a face at Rennie.

But Mariel asked: "By the way, where's the bike?"

Rennie answered, "I just leaned it over there against Alex . . . Don't worry."

"But I don't see it," she said, and shaded her eyes with her hand as she surveyed the crowds.

Rennie left her side and passed through the crowds to where Alex was standing.

"Where's the Radical?" he asked Alex.

"What do you mean? You were the one who was riding it."

"I just leaned it up against you. Didn't you notice?"

"No . . ." Alex looked around, his eyes growing large.

"But I said to you, 'Here it is,' and you put your hand back. . . . Didn't you guys see me give it to him?"

They all shook their heads at him.

"I swear, I just propped it up on you, Alex. A couple of minutes ago." Rennie's eyes were filled with fear as he turned his head from side to side, anxiously seeking out the bike. "Where is it?"

Now Mariel realized the bike was missing, and so did Robinson. Rennie, looking more frightened than Alex had ever seen him look before, was running around the crowded track, asking anyone and everyone if they had seen the bike. Some people joined in the search, combing the track, examining every bike in sight. Meanwhile, Alex's mother called the police while the announcements of winners continued as if nothing had happened. It wasn't the first time a bike had been stolen, from this track or from any other.

Some bikes were worth a thousand dollars, since they had expensive parts and invaluable frames, all collected and assembled over years as a labor of love.

"Who would be so mean, so nasty?" Mariel kept asking. "That bike was a one-of-a-kind."

The police arrived and helped them look, but little by little the track was emptying. People gave up the search as it became obvious that whoever took the bike had probably gone with it long ago.

"I hate people," Robinson said about ten times.

"How will I ever tell Dad?" Alex wondered, horrified at the very thought. "He'll kill me."

"He'll kill Rennie," Robinson corrected him.

"He won't kill anyone," said Mariel, "because it's no one's fault. These things just happen. Let's face it."

"It's Rennie's fault," Robinson insisted.

"No, it isn't. . . . And where is he, anyway?" Alex asked, wiping a tear off his face.

The last time he had seen his friend they were thrashing through bushes around the track. Rennie wore a terrible expression which showed how guilty he felt. "I'm sorry, I'm sorry," he kept saying. Now Alex couldn't see him anywhere.

"Worry about Rennie later," his mother told him. "First let's break the news to Dad."

She sighed deeply and Robinson said, "I bet you want to smoke."

"You're right," she agreed, and pulled out a cigarette.

"Let me blow out the match," the little boy insisted.

While they fiddled with matches and cigarettes, Alex

dragged ahead of them to the parking lot. His eyes brimmed with tears. He saw the big beefy man drive away in a black truck that had a license plate reading BMX RCR, and he thought of how much the man had admired the Radical.

"It can't be gone, it can't be," he whispered, but his tears fell freely.

4

Mr. Porter was not at home when they got there. He and Rosie had gone to play tennis, and left a note telling them when they would return. Alex, Robinson, and their mother changed into bathing suits and jumped into the pool; they swam around with a vengeance, too upset to talk to each other. From the history of other stolen bikes, Alex knew that it was unlikely that the police would find the Radical. He thought of trying to find it alone, and he felt helpless and very small. He was not just upset about losing the bike either.

He was scared. How would he ever tell his father, who had spent so many months trying to make the bike perfect?

Mr. Porter was not a bad-tempered man, but his stern moments could be frightening. And Alex seemed to get more than his fair share at those moments. Alex climbed to the edge of the pool, and sat there, shivering. His mother threw a towel over his back and sat down beside him.

"Don't worry," she said comfortingly. "I have a strong feeling we'll get it back."

"You do?" he asked eagerly.

"It's just a feeling. . . . Did I ever tell you about the time I had everything stolen from me?" she asked, and Alex shook his head with a look of hope in his eyes. "It was when I was a single working woman. I came home one day and my apartment was stripped bare. Nothing in it. No stereo. No TV. No radio. No bed. Nothing."

"What happened? Did you get it all back?"

"No," she said flatly. "None of it."

"So why did you tell me the story?"

"Because I *knew* I wouldn't get anything back, as soon as I saw the bare room. I had this really strong feeling: I'll never see that stuff again."

"So?" Alex said, frowning at her.

"So now I have the opposite feeling."

"Thanks a lot, Mom. That's a big help."

"Sorry, honey," she said. "I'm just trying to cheer you up."

"Well, you can't, because I really don't think I'll ever see the Radical again. Bikes don't come back. They just don't."

"Stupid Rennie," Robinson said, and stuck out his lower lip. He was floating on his back, with his water wings

42

extended to the side, and his tummy roundly looking up at the sun.

"It would be great if we could blame someone. Right?" said Mariel. "But we can't blame anyone, except the person who took it. And that's all."

"Uh-oh," Alex murmured, as the car doors slammed outside in the driveway. "Mom, you tell him."

But she looked as scared as he did, and neither of them moved. They listened and waited and finally Mr. Porter and Rosie appeared, talking about the difference between tennis and squash. Mariel stood up and linked her hand in her husband's. He was talking away to Rosie, and didn't notice everyone's expressions.

Finally Robinson rolled over in the water and bubbled: "Be quiet, Daddy."

"What?"

"Alex has something to tell you."

"What?"

"About the bike," said Robinson, and he swam with enormous splashes to the pool steps.

"What? What about the bike?" he asked.

Rosie got the look on her face which the whole family called Miss Know-It-All. Her expression became weary and cynical, while she looked at the members of her family as if they were all fools.

"I know what happened," she said slowly. "It got stolen."

"That's right!" her mother cried, as if Rosie had just won a huge prize on a talk show for answering the right question.

"Stolen?" Mr. Porter murmured questioningly.

"The new bike? But where is it now?"

"It's still stolen, Dad," Alex muttered and gulped down more tears. "It's gone."

"See? I just knew it," Rosie said. "Nothing ever works. Everything always goes wrong. I knew it."

"Wait a minute," said Mr. Porter. "Are you serious? It's really gone, Alex?"

"Yes. . . . I'm sorry!"

"Damn," said Mr. Porter under his breath. "That's a shame. A damn shame."

And he took his hand away from his wife and walked to the other side of the pool where he began to tinker automatically with the garden faucet.

His family stared at him expectantly. He often reacted to bad news by fiddling with some piece of machinery or kitchen equipment. But this time the silence dragged on, as if he was building up for an explosion. He leaned down and tightened the hose where it linked to the faucet, shook his head, then went into his shed and shut the door.

"Leave him alone for a while," said his wife, and she went inside, frowning, to start dinner. They could hear her banging pots and pans around in an abnormally clumsy way.

"I almost wish Dad would get mad," said Alex.

"Why?" asked Robinson. "I get scared when he does. I just wonder who did it. . . . I wonder if Rennie knows."

"Come on," Alex snapped.

"What?" asked Rosie. "Do you think Rennie had something to do with it being stolen?"

"No," Robinson said with a nervous glance at Alex. "But I still say he's a moto-head."

44

"Moto-head?" asked Rosie.

"He called me a brat. I hope he has a pickle stuck in his eye right now!" the little boy continued, with his cheeks puffed out from anger.

"What did Rennie do?" Rosied turned to Alex this time.

"Nothing," he told her. "So be quiet, Robinson, or I'll throw your Mongoose into the pool."

They all fell silent and stared at the shed. Finally the door shot open and Mr. Porter stood there, his face red.

"Alex!" he called. "You better make an all-out effort to get that bike back. Understand?"

For the next two days Alex did nothing but ride his old GT up and down every street in town, looking for his bike. He hung up reward signs and cross-examined every BMX racer he knew. He went all the way to Azusa under a burning sun, and asked around. But no one knew anything about the missing Radical. He asked Rennie's friend José, who lived in a huge house in the tree-lined residential part of town. José was not even interested. He was now more involved in mopeds and computers than in BMX.

"But get Rennie to help you. He's good at that kind of thing," José told Alex.

So by the end of Tuesday Alex was not only looking for the Radical, he was also looking for Rennie. He had, like the bike itself, disappeared. Alex called his home and Rennie's sister answered the phone.

"We thought he was with you," she said, and then she called into her house in Spanish.

Rennie's father came to the phone and Alex could tell

by the harshness of his breathing as he spoke that he was sick. "The last time the boy was here was Friday," he told Alex in a thick accent. "I had a call from him last night. He said he was camping out. He said he would check in. He sounded good. But I was worried. You know?"

"I'm sure he's okay," Alex said quickly. "I'll find him and tell him to get in touch with you."

"Yes, yes," the father said quickly. "His mother will be very upset if she knows he isn't with you people."

"Don't worry. He's okay, I'm sure," Alex repeated.

And he went to look for his parents because he was beginning to really worry himself.

Mariel said, "Tomorrow we'll look for him. I need his help on two cars."

Mr. Porter suggested they drive around in the morning. "I'll visit the police with you and see what they suggest."

"Thanks, Dad," Alex said, and went to help him carry some potted plants out onto the patio.

Alex couldn't sleep that night, worrying. When all the lights in the house were out, and it was after midnight, he checked the sky and saw it was illuminated by a nearly full moon. He put on some clothes and snuck out the side door, mounted his GT, and rode through the silent streets to the state park where Rennie camped out. He was scared. The mountains loomed, black and threatening, against the dim sky. It was so different riding late at night than during the day. The state park seemed like a place he might visit in a nightmare. The trail was thin and bordered by brambles. Crickets made a noise as loud and complicated as a symphony orchestra. And some creature was making hollow, hooting noises.

Alex half rode and half pushed his bike down the trail to the clearing. It was lighted by the moon, but was tinted the color of steel, an unnatural color. He pushed his bike across the grass to the place where Rennie camped.

There was no one there.

No sign of disturbed grass, no leftover objects. Nothing.

Alex was now breathing high in his chest, and he felt very alone in that clearing under the wide sky. He wanted to be at home in bed, immediately, without having to go to all the trouble of getting there.

Where had Rennie gone?

He guessed that it was guilt and shame that had made Rennie disappear, and he wanted to tell him to forget it. *Everything is okay,* he wanted to say. *Nobody blames you.*

But there was no Rennie.

Dejected and uneasy, he hurried back to the trail and pushed his way by brambles and branches as fast as he could until he returned to the main road. Then he sped home on his GT in the moonlight, and no one even knew that he had been gone.

Wednesday, near noon, Alex's father kept his promise and they set off for the police station. Robinson insisted on coming too and sat in the back seat, playing with a couple of G.I. Joe dolls.

"Boom . . . pow . . . c-r-r-rack," he sounded from the back.

Alex was biting his nails and dreading seeing the inside of the station; it made his problem seem so important.

"Alex," said his father out of the blue. "Are you sure Rennie doesn't know more about this than we think?"

"What would he know?" asked Alex. "He'd tell us."

"I don't understand why he's been avoiding us then."

"I got an idea," Robinson suddenly announced.

"I bet you do," Alex mumbled in a grumpy voice.

"Let's see if Rennie's at Taco Bell."

"Don't be dumb."

"You're dumb, bumble-bee brain."

"If he was at Taco Bell, I'd know it. It's too obvious," Alex said.

"Well, let's just take a look before we go to the police," Mr. Porter said. "You never know."

Robinson climbed up on his knees excitedly, and looked out the window.

"I just bet you he's there," he said.

"Well, I don't."

"You think you're so great, Alex. I really, really hate you."

"Shh, boys," warned Mr. Porter. "No fighting."

They pulled up in front of Taco Bell, and Alex went in alone, a blush of embarrassment on his face. It seemed like the stupidest idea in the world, just because it was Robinson's. And there was Addie Sparks at the counter, smiling under the fluorescent lights.

"Hi, Alex," she said cheerfully. "Looking for Rennie?"

"Sort of. You seen him?"

"He's back in the kitchen. Can you believe it? He got a job here, as a cook."

"You're kidding."

"No. Why would I be?"

"Can I go see him?" asked Alex.

"Sure, go ahead."

Alex went through the swinging door, his eyes wide with disbelief. There was Rennie in a white apron, rolling out tortillas, and stuffing them. When he saw Alex, he looked startled and guilty.

"Rennie, I've been looking for you everywhere. Have you been hanging around here all this time?"

"Man, I'm sorry," said Rennie. "I went and hid out somewhere for a couple of days. Then I had to eat, and I came here, and Addie said I could get this job . . . I'm sorry. Really. And I bet the bike is still gone, and it's my fault."

Alex looked at his friend and stifled the anger he was feeling. It was like a piece of his worry turning into something else, something bitter. He had never been angry at Rennie before, but the lonely trip the night before had scared him. And now he felt mad that Rennie didn't tell him where he was hiding out, or try to contact him, or help him find the bike.

"The bike's still gone," Alex admitted, "but I've been everywhere looking. Thanks for the help."

"Wow, I'm sorry, Alex," Rennie said, and his face showed his apology.

"And your family is really worried. And my mother needs your help on two cars . . . And if Addie will let you, maybe you can tear yourself away one of these days and help me try to find the bike." Alex's heart was knocking on his chest and his head ached. He left the restaurant and jumped into the car.

"He's there," he told his father.

Robinson let out a squeal of self-satisfaction and rolled around the back seat, squeaking like a piglet, his knees up in the air.

"At least we know he's okay," said Mr. Porter.

Alex didn't respond, but sank down in the seat, glowering. He wished he hadn't gotten quite so mad at Rennie, and he hated letting Robinson get the last laugh.

His father seemed to understand, because he looked over his shoulder and said, "Shut up," at Robinson, which was something he hardly ever said. Alex felt better immediately, and Robinson stopped giggling at once.

As they headed toward the police station, Alex told his father, "Rennie doesn't know anything. He blames it on himself."

Mr. Porter replied, "Oh, I'm sure he does. Wouldn't you?"

Alex nodded and didn't much like the feeling that his father might know more about this kind of thing than he did.

"Well, I want to let the police know that this is a case of patent theft. Not just another BMX theft. They ought to know that."

"It won't make any difference," Alex muttered.

He was a little embarrassed by his father's self-assurance and, even though he hoped it might work wonders on the police, something in Alex made him feel convinced that they would not care what kind of theft it was.

"That was an original," Mr. Porter said emphatically.

They pulled up in front of the brick building, shaded by leafy trees. Inside, at the desk, Mr. Porter told the sergeant the story and how the bike might be worth a good deal of money.

"Most of them are," said the sergeant who looked as bored by Mr. Porter as he had by Alex. "They're all worth money. Kids dump hundreds into parts for those things. Ridiculous. You'll be lucky if you see one tire of it again."

"But the parts on my bike wouldn't fit on any other," said Mr. Porter. "Don't you understand? This was an invention, one of a kind."

"You should've patented it before you let the boy bring it to the track, if it was so special," said the sergeant.

Mr. Porter gave Alex a long stern look. Then he asked: "What kind of person steals a bike, in most cases?"

"A kid who has less things than others. . . . A kid who can't afford to buy even a cheap one. . . . Someone who feels like an outsider. You know, not part of the racing scene . . . Someone who needs money."

"I see," Mr. Porter said seriously. "Well, I'd appreciate your paying special attention to this case."

"Sure," said the sergeant with a nod.

He looked at Alex and Alex looked at him and both of them knew that the police couldn't do anything at all to retrieve the Radical.

5

That same afternoon, Rennie arrived and got to work on the two cars in the driveway. Mariel was quick to forgive him for disappearing. She needed his help. The two cars needed minor repairs and she had minor equipment, and Rennie was especially skilled at getting deep inside an engine without twisting himself into knots in the process. They never said much to each other when they worked, and this time they said even less. She didn't want to embarrass him by asking all kinds of questions about where he had been. Especially with Addie Sparks sitting on a rock beside the driveway, blasting New Wave music from her box.

Alex had hoped to talk to Rennie, but now he saw that it was impossible. So he rode off on his bike to Pete's house and spent the rest of the afternoon playing basketball in the park. Alex was racking his brain, all the time trying to think up a way to find his bike. It was like a tune he couldn't get out of his head. Every time he saw the flash of silver and heard the whir of spokes, he spun around to see if the Radical was passing by.

"Pay attention!" Pete called to him.

And he tried to, but finally he sat on a bench in the shade, where he could think in peace and watch the others play.

Rick rode up on a ten-speed. He was, for once, alone.

"Hi, Alex," he said, and sat down beside him as if they were good friends. "What's up?"

"Nothing."

"I passed your house. Saw Addie out there."

"Yeah?"

"Yeah. I guess she and your friend are going together?"

"No, they're not. She just follows him around," said Alex, and leaned down to tighten the laces on his sneakers.

Rick was wearing what the wealthy kids wore: black-checked Vans with no laces. He laughed and said: "Addie follows him around? That's a joke."

"Listen," said Alex, eager to change the subject, "my bike got stolen last weekend. At Azusa."

"What bike? You're sitting with one."

"No, my new one, the one my father built for me. A beautiful silver bike. You couldn't miss it, because there isn't another one in the world like it. . . . Will you please keep your eye out for it?"

Rick stared at Alex as if he was just seeing him for the first time. His jaw was clenched when he asked, "That was your bike?"

"You saw it, huh?"

"Yeah, I thought it was Pancho Villa's."

"His name is Rennie. And no. It was mine."

"Well, how did it get stolen?" Rick asked.

"Rennie handed it over to me, and I wasn't paying attention—"

"*You* weren't!" Rick shouted a laugh. "Boy, Alex, you sure are dumb."

"What do you mean?"

"Rennie *says* you weren't paying attention. How do you know *he* didn't steal it?"

Alex just smiled and shook his head. "Rennie would never do that."

"Really? I know for a fact that his father can't pay his medical bills and the family is on food stamps."

"So what? That doesn't turn him into a thief."

Rick climbed on his bike, balanced there, and gave Alex a look to show how superior he was.

"You sure are loyal—and dumb, like a dog," he said, and rode away.

Alex watched him go and then left himself. The sky was getting dusky and the smog was thick against the wall of mountains to the west. In ten days he was going to race in Laguna, and all his dreams of winning on the Radical were gone. He felt he had no future in BMX without the Radical. And he was beginning to feel his future with Rennie was clouded. Rick's attitude had made him remember what the police sergeant said about what kind of person steals a bike: "A kid who has less things than others. . . . Someone who feels like an outsider. . . . Someone who needs money."

"But no," Alex told himself quickly. "It would never be Rennie."

It was Addie Sparks who came up with the idea that they go see her cousin who owned a bike store in the next town over.

"Bikes are his business," she insisted. "He might know something."

"It's worth a try, I guess," said Alex, and he looked at Rennie to see what his reaction was.

They were all sitting on the curb outside Alex's house while the evening sprinklers spouted up and down the street and the smell of smoke from the barbecue wafted around them.

"I don't know," said Rennie. "What could he tell us, if he just sells new bikes?"

"You've got to promise never ever, ever to tell anyone in school about him," said Addie solemnly.

"Why not?"

Addie grew a little pink at Rennie's question, and her eyes glittered. "If kids knew I was related to someone like him, they'd think I was jail bait or something. They'd never speak to me again."

"What for?" asked Rennie.

"I promise I won't tell," Alex said quickly.

Rennie shrugged. "I guess I'll promise too."

"Okay," said Addie, and she automatically lowered her

voice to a whisper, even though no one was around. "He's pretty sleazy. He goes to Las Vegas all the time, to gamble, and he's had three wives. My mom says he never gives any child support to any of his kids."

"He sounds pretty clever," Rennie said with a grin. "How do we get there?"

She put up her thumb: "Car, bike, or hike."

Alex thought he ought to say that his parents would never allow him to hitchhike, but he also didn't want to sound like a baby.

"On the freeway?" Rennie asked.

"No, you can go by Foothill, and about a mile after The Mall you come to Manzanita on your right. It goes down toward the valley."

"What's the store called?"

"Manzanita Bike Shop. He's really imaginative, right? It's down that street on your left."

"Maybe he'll take me to Vegas. I could sure use some money," said Rennie.

"Sure," she said with sarcasm, and smiled so dimples appeared in her cheeks. "Actually you'd be surprised how much money he makes gambling. But never mind that. Just say you know me."

"A lot of good that will do," Rennie muttered.

As he spoke, a breeze sent water from the sprinkler showering all over his back. It made Addie laugh hysterically and Alex jump to his feet. By then the dark had covered everything in sight, and Rennie offered to ride Addie home on his bike. Alex started to ask Rennie if he wanted to come back, but he figured his friend was now the property of Addie Sparks and he'd better get used to it. Anyway, she wasn't all that bad.

" 'Night, you guys," he said.

"See you after work tomorrow!" Rennie called. "And we'll head for Manzanita, pronto!"

The following day, in the late afternoon, Rennie arrived on a moped. It was fire-engine red and silver and gleamed like a Christmas bulb in the cooling sun.

"Hop on," he told Alex.

"Are you serious?"

"Your mom wouldn't want you thumbing a ride," he explained. "So I borrowed this from José."

"Wow!" Alex whooped with pleasure and climbed on the moped behind Rennie. "Cool!"

They rumbled away, toward the high and smoggy wall of mountains. The mountain they approached was called La Caputa—the Hood—because it looked exactly like a brown monk's hood, and you could even see, in a certain evening light, the features of a man in the rock formation. It looked like his eyes were closed in prayer and he had a very long nose, which was actually a ledge beside a ravine that was covered with sagebrush. Some said he looked like a she—a witch in a pointed cap.

Rennie and Alex biked on a cement road which wound west along the base of La Caputa and toward the next town. Two blocks away they could see houses, shopping malls, and cars, but Rennie preferred to get used to the moped on a quieter road. In about a quarter of an hour they left the mountain behind. A couple of cars passed them, and Rennie had to turn away from this peaceful route to enter town, the main boulevards, and the traffic.

"There's The Mall," he announced.

The air began to smell of oil and gas fumes. Traffic lights shone for a couple of miles until they disappeared in a mist of heat and smog. Along the sides of the street there were a series of little malls. But they knew what Addie meant by The Mall. It was one enormous concrete building, with cars glittering for acres around it. This was the place where kids hung out on weekends, during the school year.

Manzanita, the street beyond The Mall, was also lined with stores. Alex always wondered how so many stores could have enough customers. His, Robinson's, and Rosie's favorite store sold jars and jars of penny candy: jelly bears, jelly beans, jelly fish, butter creams, gumdrops, chocolate kisses, caramels, raspberries, licorice, butterscotch, turtles, sourballs, and many others. However, the moped shot right past that store and turned to park in front of Manzanita Bike Shop. In the window were the standard ten-speeds, along with one Hutch. Through the glass, Alex saw rows and rows of bikes for sale, some on raised platforms, others on the floor.

At the back of the store, making change for a customer, was Addie's cousin. He was around thirty, with slicked-back hair that looked dyed blond, and a tanned, smiling face. He wore a flowered safari shirt and Bermuda shorts. The bell rang on the door as it shut behind Rennie and Alex.

They looked at the bikes, so beautiful in so many small and important ways, and their eyes filled with envy. Very thin tires for racing contrasted with the fat dirt-bike tires, but each was grand in its own way.

"Can I help you boys?" the cousin called as the customer left the store.

"Hi, yeah," said Rennie. "We're friends of Addie's—Addie Sparks."

"Addie's a great kid," said the cousin as he came toward them, a smile pasted across a set of large, perfect teeth. "She always cracks me up. Those freckles! That hair! And she has the temper to go along with them. Have you seen her get mad?"

"Not yet," said Rennie.

"Well, when you do, take my advice and run."

Alex and Rennie shot fake smiles back at him. Then Alex spoke.

"See, my bike was stolen at a racetrack a couple of days ago, and Addie said you might have some ideas how to find it."

"I personally have about five secondhand bikes for sale," the cousin said through his smile. "They've all been here for a few weeks. I don't like dealing in secondhand. You understand. But go look at them if you want."

His smile was beginning to get tired, and Rennie wandered past him to look at the used bikes. Only two were BMX.

"I love kids," the man said to Alex. "Addie's got quite a large family. Have you met her brothers and sisters?"

Alex was thinking about how he never paid child support, when Rennie shouted, "Hey! This looks like Nick's Red Line! It got stolen out of his backyard."

The cousin's smile was completely exhausted now, and he walked to the back of the store, saying, "That's why I don't like dealing in secondhand. Someone always claims it's stolen property. These are legitimate sales. If someone thinks this is his, then let him come in and prove it. You should always register your bikes in the police station."

"I'll tell Nick to come and look at it," said Rennie. "He was pretty upset about losing it. It's not like he can just go out and buy a new one."

The cousin shot a dirty look at Rennie and turned to Alex. "What kind of bike did you lose?" he asked.

Alex described the bike.

"Boy, I'd like to see it. Sounds real special. . . . My advice is this, boys. Check out every bike store between here and Pasadena, run an ad in the local paper offering a reward, and—and—that's it!"

"Thanks," Rennie growled.

Alex said good-bye for them both, and they stepped into the heat again.

"Shoot," said Rennie. "I gotta tell Nick about his bike. I'm sure that was his."

"I guess we better do what the man said and just keep going to stores."

"Fine with me. I'll help whenever I can. Maybe to-morrow afternoon around this time? I can usually get the moped off José then."

"I'll look around, too, alone," said Alex.

They got on the moped again and, as they sped into the

line of traffic, Alex felt a little rise in his hopes, since the bike stores did get stolen bikes after all.

The next day Alex asked his father if he could use his ten-speed bike to go search for the Radical. Mr. Porter was in the shed fixing one Ken and two Barbie dolls for Rosie. Their pink heads and legs and arms were lying on the workbench, and their torsos were lined up with pliers and wire. Rosie was seated in an old armchair in the corner. The armchair was her favorite nest on all of their property. She practiced her violin and read there. Her father had fixed up a little reading light and some shelves for her, where she wouldn't be in his way or too close to machinery.

"You can borrow my bike," Mr. Porter said to Alex, as he stared inside Ken's empty torso through the hole where his neck had been. "But you have to borrow the lock too—and use it."

"I will. I promise."

"Where are you going?"

"I've got a list of bike stores. I'll go to as many as I can."

"The more time that passes, the less chance you have of finding it," Rosie said.

Alex made a face at her, thanked his father, and left.

Indoors he had a dull and hopeless feeling, but as soon as he was on his father's bike, alone, that feeling left him. He shot down the hill with the wind on his face, and then pedaled along a quiet street for several blocks till he turned down toward the strip of shopping malls.

There he found a bike store called The Silver Spoke. He locked his father's bike outside where he could see it and went in. Classical music was playing from the back area. He could see right away that this was a store which catered to older bikers and not BMX. Fancy hiking equipment was displayed alongside the elegant racers. From the back of the store stepped a large, silver-haired man dressed in blue denims, a pipe in his hand. He smiled at Alex.

"You look like you've made a mistake," he said pleasantly.

"I'm actually looking for a more BMX-type store," Alex told him.

"That you can find down Foothill, two blocks in the Hearthstone Plaza."

Alex turned to the door to leave, but the man spoke again.

"If you're looking for secondhand, your best bet is in Belle Grande. There's a store there called the Bike Exchange. The man is into buying used bikes. BMX especially."

"Thanks. I'll try that."

Alex took one more look into the store he was in and made a mental note to tell his father about it. What with the classical music and the fancy equipment, it was just his father's idea of a perfect bike store.

Then he moved on to the Heartstone Plaza, where he had no luck, and to two other stores, where he also had no luck, and finally, hot and tired, he cycled home. It was already Friday, the bike had been gone five days, and he felt no closer to it than he had the day he lost it.

At home his mother gave him a glass of lemonade while he fixed a sandwich. She said, "I'll put an ad in the paper for you today, honey. But I guess you should still go to the bike stores and post some more reward signs."

"Rennie and I will go out later," he told her, biting into a ham sandwich that dripped mustard. He looked at her and wondered if he should mention his slight suspicion about Rennie.

"Yes, I do think Ren should help as much as he can. It's partly his fault," she said. "I hate to say it, but it is."

"I wonder why he wasn't paying more attention," Alex said in a low voice, half hoping she didn't hear.

"No one's perfect," was her response. "Now, listen. I'm going to need you to babysit a couple of times in the coming days. And we've got a race tomorrow too."

"Babysit?" Alex groaned.

"I know. I'm sorry. But there are things I have to do, and we were invited to a barbecue."

"Okay. Just tell me when so I can get ready."

"It's not that bad. I might even pay you."

Alex dropped the crust of his sandwich into the garbage and wandered out to the patio to read and wait for Rennie. He could hear the screech-scrawch of Rosie's violin from inside the shed, and the hum of his father's machine. He went back inside and stayed in his room where it was quiet.

Later that afternoon, Rennie arrived on the moped as he promised. Alex climbed on.

"José is so lucky," Rennie said. "His family is loaded but he's not stingy. He lets me use this whenever he can."

"You really like riding it, don't you?" said Alex.

"Like it isn't the word. I'm going to get one of these for myself."

"I thought you were going to get a GT," Alex said, surprised.

"Uh-uh . . . No more BMX," said Rennie.

"Why not?"

"I don't know. It's hard to explain. It's expensive, for one thing. And also I feel sort of dumb there, like an outsider. What's the point. I don't like crowds."

"An outsider?" Alex wondered.

"Don't worry about it," said Rennie. "I'm saving up some money. What I don't give to my dad. I'll get one of these. You'll see."

"I guess I will," said Alex, and then he directed Rennie to the Bicycle Exchange in Belle Grande.

The owner of this store was a small, elfinlike man with a pointed chin that seemed to be trying to reach the pointed nose hanging down over it. His profile reminded Alex of La Caputa. He had a few teeth, but not many, and he wore workclothes layered in grease. The cloth was so stiff it crackled as he moved. There was a fat, blond lady at the back of the store, working over piles of bills. She was drinking light beer and smoking mentholated cigarettes.

The store itself was heaped with bicycles, all of them piled against and on top of each other. There was little light inside, so it was hard to tell what color each bike was. But Rennie started pulling up handlebars and looking anyway.

The woman was talking aloud, but not to the man with

the pointed chin. He was talking to Rennie and Alex, so it looked as if she was just talking to herself. There was no one around her, just an open door into a dark area.

"BMX is the greatest sport to come down the pike," the elfin man said excitedly. "Never saw nothing like the way it's spreading—even to Japan and, maybe soon, to the Olympics. And when you think it started in the old backyard. Never would've believed . . . What you boys looking for?"

"A really special bike," said Rennie, "called the Radical."

"Never hear of one of them. What about you, Hal?"

They turned to look at the woman who was still talking. She said something about putting cinnamon in her applesauce, when a man came partway out of the dark room. The boys could only tell that he wasn't very large, and he was well dressed.

"What say?" he called.

"A bike called the Radical . . . Every heard of one?"

"Never," said the man and disappeared again.

"That's Hal. He'd know too. He's a factory sponsor. I get lots of them coming in here, but he's an old friend. I'm teaching him some repair tricks in that room. I get people from GT, Schwinn, Rainbow. The guy from Rainbow. You know him? He's a fixture around the local tracks."

"I think so," said Alex, still staring through the gloom at the dark, empty doorway.

"The man from Rainbow is a bigshot, or thinks he is, anyway. Works the graveyard shift. Ha! Hear that, Candy? I said Paul works the graveyard shift." He began to chuckle with his mouth an open hole, like the dark room in the back, and even Rennie stopped looking at bikes to stare at him. "Hear that, Hal?" he called.

This time there was no response from Hal. The fat woman called out instead, "Your jokes are about as appetizing as cold pizza. Come on back and help me with this ledger."

The man said, "Go on, boys. Poke around to your heart's content. But you aren't going to find no Radical. Got plenty of conservatives. But no radicals. Ha-ha-ha!"

"I think you're right about that," Rennie muttered. "Let's go, Alex."

They went back into the sun, very discouraged.

"That place was really creepy," said Alex.

"It should be called The Robber's Den."

"I bet half the stolen bikes in the area are in there."

"The other half," said Rennie, "he's already stripped or spray-painted, and sold. . . . Wow. I thought those chop shops were for cars only. I tell you, I'm going to get myself a moped and forget bikes."

"I can't," said Alex. "I love BMX. And I won't rest till my bike is back."

"We'll keep at it. Don't worry," said Rennie.

But Alex was reaching the stage where he couldn't be comforted.

6

The next day Alex's mother took him, Robinson, Rosie, Pete, and a couple of other friends to the race at a track south of where they lived. Rennie stayed behind. He told Alex to keep racing the old GT, just to keep in shape.

"I honestly bet you'll never find that bike," Rosie said.

"Come on, Rosie," Rennie said. "You've got to have faith!"

"Are you going to do more looking?" Alex asked.

"Yes, but I won't if you don't promise to bring home a trophy. I mean, you've got to keep racing or you'll get out of shape and you won't be able to ride the Radical right, when we get it back."

Alex knew that Rennie was just trying to make him feel better. It didn't work. A big part of him just wanted to stay home and continue searching with Rennie. But a little part also hoped that he would see someone riding the Radical at the track. He didn't say this to anyone, but kept it secret, as if it would be stronger that way.

"I'm going to whip you today," his friend Pete announced as they sped down the freeway. "With your old GT you're no better than anyone else."

"That's not true," Alex retorted. "Before I had the Radical, I could beat you without trying, and you know it."

They were joking. Pete just rode BMX for fun, like a lot of kids did. He wasn't seriously committed to the sport, the way Alex was, and he wasn't half as skilled.

"You better not beat Alex," said Robinson. "He's already in a bad mood. See how his cowlick is sticking up? That means he's grumpy."

Alex smoothed down his hair and they all laughed. Robinson was sitting up front with his mother. She wouldn't let him touch the radio dials because he always wanted to listen to country-western, which he called "cowboy singing," and it made her sad.

"Let's take the coast road," she said over the clear voice of Boy George.

They cut through the brownish hills and soon came out onto the freeway which gave them quick glimpses of the green and gray Pacific Ocean. Lush gardens hid behind fences and trees. This was a rich section of Southern California, and the ocean looked dazzling behind a spray of pink flowers.

70

Occasionally a car buried in BMX bikes would roll by them, obviously on its way to the same race. The track was called Star Track, because most of the best races, the Nationals, were held there, with bikers from all over the country coming to race and camp out.

Alex was staring out the window, daydreaming about finding the Radical at this race, when he saw a familiar black truck. It pulled out in front of them, racing at high speed in the left lane. There were at least three people inside.

The license plate on the truck was BMX RCR.

"Hey, Mom, there goes that man from Rainbow Toys. Remember? I think he might want to sponsor me."

"Great," she commented. "It's getting to be that time."

To Alex, having a sponsor meant growing up, being independent, making his own money, becoming professional, and doing what he loved to do in a whole new way. It meant riding a bike *for* someone, not just himself; it meant being in magazines; it meant traveling with strangers instead of his mother. He had, for a couple of years, dreamed of the day when a sponsor would approach him at a race. Now he actually saw it coming, and it meant almost nothing without the Radical.

"I'm going to be a surfer when I grow up," said Robinson, looking out the window at the sea.

"That's great, Robinson. You want to be a beach bum?" Pete exclaimed, grinning.

"Yes . . . I want to be a beach bum," said Robinson very seriously. But Alex could tell, by the little boy's expression, that he didn't know what he was talking about.

It wasn't until they got out on the track grounds, though,

71

and they were unpacking their truck, that he saw who the people in the black truck were. Besides the sponsor were Rick, Jeff, and Stu.

There was really no reason for Alex to be surprised by this fact, but he was anyway. He figured that the man wanted those guys on his team. Alex watched them pulling out their bikes, one after the other, while the man stood back, too well dressed to touch a greasy bike. The smell of cologne wafted over Alex.

"Hi, Alex," called Stu. "It's going to be a mob scene here!"

The area was already jammed with cars and campers and there were signs of people who were planning to stay for the whole weekend. Tents and barbecue equipment were set up in the camping section beyond the track. There were two ambulances, and a couple of policemen beside the stand. There was a store for BMX equipment, and a concession stand that looked permanent. The Star Track was definitely a pro's ideal place to race.

"Hey, kid, what class are you racing?" the sponsor asked Alex, as they walked to the track together.

"Twelve-expert," Alex told him, and tried not to sound overeager.

"If you make it to the mains, I'll be keeping an eye on you. Where's your bike?"

"You mean the Radical? It was stolen."

Alex was instantly depressed. He didn't listen to the sponsor's reaction, but jumped on his GT and rode away. Alone, he could focus on checking out the bikes that were there. Hundreds of them. He pushed his GT in and out of crowds of people, looking carefully at every bike he

72

could, but there was no sign of the Radical. He tried now to concentrate on the racing itself

"What a piggy man," were his mother's first words when she found him.

"I didn't like him either," Robinson agreed. "Yag! He smells of perfume."

"Who are you talking about?" asked Alex.

"The sponsor, dum-dum."

"Oh, yeah. Well, just don't be rude to him," Alex told his brother, who looked up to see what the cowlick was doing.

Soon they all forgot about the sponsor, they were so busy registering, passing inspection, and getting into line for their motos. The best racers in the country were there, Alex noted, and he went around with Robinson, who wanted to get the autographs of the pros. Alex recognized one face after another, either from magazines or from previous races. But when he saw Pat and Mark, he went the other way, so they wouldn't know he still didn't have the Radical. Around the clusters of top riders were sponsors from factories and bike stores, and Alex even thought he recognized Hal, the man from the back room at the Bike Exchange store. When he saw him, he paused, wondering. The man was short and well dressed, with a pleasant face. It was hard for Alex to connect him with the elfin owner of the store, who seemed so criminal.

"The pros don't look all that great," Robinson said in a loud voice, right near a group of them. Alex gave him a dirty look and Robinson quickly added, "I mean, they look normal,"

"Well, what did you expect?" Alex asked.

"Rich people," said Robinson.

Alex made his aren't-you-stupid face, and pushed his brother into a small cluster of pros. Robinson walked around, from one to the other, with his pencil and paper raised in the air and his eyes lowered to the ground.

Watching, Alex remembered how surprised he was, too, when he found out his heroes were normal people, or just like him. They were kids who came from regular families and who learned BMX in their backyards and on the streets. Most of the original tracks were set up and run by parents, like Alex's mother, and racing was a weekend, family operation. It was mainly for fun. A dirt bike was a dirt bike and not BMX, in the beginning. It was a slow process, learning what great moves you could make on those little fat-wheeled bikes. Alex learned with his friends how to do tabletops and wheelies on mounds of abandoned construction dirt.

Now BMX was a business. In that huge, hot crowd, with the music blasting and people at a fever pitch about winning or losing, Alex could hardly remember what it felt like to ride for fun. His stomach was beginning to churn, nervously, and he pulled Robinson through the crowds in their mother's direction, eager to get rid of him.

"You better win, stupid," Robinson said to him.

"If I just had the Radical I know I would," Alex said with a sigh.

All at once a hand fell on his shoulder. It belonged to the sponsor from Rainbow Toys. Alex looked up his wide belly, cased in a green polyester shirt, to his thick face.

"Alex," he said. "If you do good today, I want to talk

to you seriously, about a possible sponsorship. . . . Folks
tell me you're something else. Even on the GT, and not
just the—what did you call it again? I keep forgetting."

"The Radical," Alex told him, with his heart pounding.

"The Radical, eh? Oh yes, I guess you told me that the
last time we met. Your father gave it to you?"

"Actually," Alex began proudly, "my dad—"

At that moment Robinson punched Alex in the stomach, and stared up at him with a red and furious face.

"Hey, what's wrong with you?" Alex asked.

"Moto-head. Mommy's going to kill you."

"My brother is a jerk," Alex said apologetically.

But then his friends shouted at him to come stand in
line, and the man backed away. Alex gave Robinson a
mean look.

"Thanks a lot. You may just have ruined my chances
to get a sponsor."

And he walked away with his GT and his helmet and
joined his friends. A tear rolled down Robinson's dusty
cheek, and his mother came to him and wiped it off. Alex
watched. He felt guilty because his nervousness had made
him act so rotten to Robinson. He wished that his mother
would come and tell him to relax and forget about winning.
He wished she would tell him to have a good time, the
way she used to. Instead he saw her stomp out her cigarette and move in his direction with a frown.

"Stop being so nasty to your brother," she scolded.

"Sorry," said Alex.

"Now get a good start, and watch that second berm.
You should be on the inside when you take it. Okay?"

"Okay, Mom."

They both looked at the crowd and the track, and for a minute she didn't say anything. But as Alex's moto moved forward toward the gate, she looked at him and winked.

"Above all," she said, "have a good time."

And she walked back to join Robinson. Alex felt better, immediately. He wanted to win for Robinson who was excitedly moving into a space where he could watch the whole race. And he wanted to win for Rennie.

Finally at the gate, he got a good start and followed his mother's instructions. They turned out to be right. A collision on the second berm took out three bikers and Alex came in first by staying on the inside and avoiding the pile-up with an agile swerve of the wheel. As usual, 12 experts had three separate races. But today there were so many listed in that category, that the winners would have to race each other in the mains.

In the meantime he watched Robinson race with five little boys. Two fell down right away, so Robinson was in the lead. But then he shot right over the side of the second berm and landed in the bushes. Everyone shouted and laughed, while the two other little boys, now in the lead, looked back to see where Robinson disappeared. They got their pedals stuck in their whirring spokes and crashed. They sat there, looking confused, while Robinson crawled out of the bushes, dragging his bike, and continued the race. Covered with leaves and thistles, his helmet lopsided, he came in first. It was the comic relief of the day.

"Watch this boy annihilate the trophy chasers . . . José Garcia gets tangled, almost goes off the track—but no, he's back . . . and look at Alex Porter go—a madman if I ever saw one, jumping suicide-style. . . . Uh-oh. José's getting squirrely. He's gonna holeshot Alex, make him go overboard . . . Uh-oh. No way, says Alex. He must be aiming for the mains and after that a factory . . . He's coming up to moonwalk . . . speed-jumps first and last, he takes a beautiful double-jump—look at him go! He's in first by a long shot. . . . Alex, I bet you'll be riding for a factory by the end of the day."

Alex came in first in his third race of the day, and was set to ride in the mains. He was breathless and hot, and he took off his racing shirt to cool off. His mother went to get him a Coke, and Robinson, eating a hamburger, joined him in the little patch of shade they found.

Alex saw the sponsor pushing through the crush of bikes and people. He was coming in their direction, and his forehead glistened with perspiration. He was red in his ears and cheeks, and smiling broadly.

"Hey there, Alex. You sure did beautiful. Made the others look zip-doodley-squat."

"Thanks," said Alex.

"Zip what?" asked Robinson, squinting way up at the man.

"Zip-doodley-squat, shh," Alex whispered fast, but it didn't stop Robinson. He said the three words out loud and burst into laughter, with his mouth spilling hamburger.

"Where's your mother?" the man asked.

Alex pointed her out.

"I want to talk to her about your future, like I mentioned before. . . . You interested?"

"Sure," said Alex.

"Well, listen, kid. I guess by now you know what it entails. You begin to travel with the pros. You win money." He mopped sweat off his face with a handkerchief, staring at Alex's mother while he talked.

"Zip-doodley squat!" Robinson gurgled, and he rolled on his back laughing.

"Ask my mom what she thinks," Alex told the sponsor, who nodded and wandered over to the stand where Mariel stood.

Alex watched them talk and tried to make Robinson be quiet at the same time. Then he got so mad at his little brother, who couldn't stop giggling, he jumped up and left him there.

The man was saying, "You must know you have a champion on your hands. That's why you've been taking him around and getting involved. There might be a lot of money—"

"No, that's not why," Alex's mother said emphatically and sipped from the Coke she had bought for him.

"Yeah? Then why?"

"We started small, with a track in an abandoned lot near our house. Myself and some other parents, we just got it together for the fun of it, for the kids . . . We never dreamed it would all get so big and commercial."

"Well, but here it is. Big and commercial," the sponsor said, looking around. "You gotta swing with it. Right?"

78

Alex saw his mother trying to think up a good come-back, as she drank his Coke. Before she could speak, the sponsor said, "And speaking of commercial, that bike, the one that got ripped, could you tell me a little bit about it? Like where you got it. Japan? West Germany, maybe?"

"My husband made it," she told him with pride. "It was beautiful, huh?"

"No kidding . . . Well, I'd sure like to know what he put into it, what kind of metals, you know, to make it so lightweight. . . . Is it covered, legally, I mean, so no one can steal the idea from him?"

"Those are big questions," she replied, and held more tightly onto the cup of Coke while Alex tried to twist it out of her hand. "I don't have the answers to them."

"I do," said Alex quickly, and as soon as he did, she spilled the Coke onto his bare stomach, and he yelped.

"Uh-oh. Sorry, honey. Better go get a napkin," she said, and gave him a shove.

The man went on talking as if nothing had happened.

"You think your husband plans to sell it to a factory? The idea, I mean?"

"We're not talking about it. Not until Alex's bike is back at home," she told him. "I better go help Alex get ready for the mains."

The man followed her to where Alex was mopping off his stomach.

"Well now, Alex," he said, "if you decide to let us sponsor you, I sure hope you'll think of giving us the magic ingredient for that bike of yours." He then reached into his pocket, got out his wallet, and handed Mariel his card.

"Here's my name and number. Give me a call when you both decide. Time for the mains now. Way to go, Alex, way to go."

And he walked back into the crowd, smiling.

"Thanks for spilling my Coke, Mom," said Alex. "I really did want to cool off."

"I'm sorry, honey, but you were about to let him know too much. After all, your father didn't patent the design to the bike, which means anyone can copy the design. Get what I mean? He better do something about that. Fast."

Alex slipped on his shirt and went to get the GT for the final stage of the day's racing. Robinson was sitting with all of their bikes and a couple of other little boys. They all had their chins in their hands and looked very glum.

"Boy, your mood sure changed fast, Rob. What's wrong?" asked Alex.

"What a bummer," the little boy sighed. "I'm not even getting a third."

"How do you know?"

"Pepe looked at the list. None of us is getting a trophy. What a bummer."

Alex told them he was sorry and went to get in line for the final race of the day. He was going against six other 12 experts who were also capable of becoming pros. One of them, Billy Williams, was the brother of the guy who had just won pro money, pro National and pro open. This kid, Billy, was real competition to Alex, and he was already sponsored by a factory.

They had a short wait and then the gate went down,

and Alex saw nothing but the track, brown and shimmering in the heat. Down the starting hill, he was neck and neck with Billy Williams.

The announcer's voice was like someone chasing him:

"Billy's got the snap on Alex, he's gaining the lead, and Roger is letting a charging Tommy by to avoid a tangle on the berm . . . Look at that William Williams go. Like his brother, eh? Greg just got his second pro open win this year . . . And now his brother's in the heat with Alex Porter standing tall, and aiming to win, too . . ."

Alex pedaled like a maniac, not looking to his left or right. He could feel Billy's bike beside him, then a little ahead, then a little behind, and going around the berms Billy got a big lead by crowding him. Their handlebars almost knocked. They went over the hill together, down, and across the track to the final whoop-de-dos, and Alex heard the crowds cheering and screaming as they flew high in the air together, landed together, and shot to the finish, with Billy in the lead by three inches.

It was a great race, one of the best ever, and Alex rushed over to say so to Billy. They were both out of breath, and their faces were dusty and grinning. They talked to each other quickly about how it had been a beautiful few minutes.

"You did great," Billy told him.

Alex thanked him but thought, "I would've won if I had had the Radical."

"Good race, Porter . . ."

"Great going, kid . . ."

Stu, Rick, and Jeff patted his back as he walked by. He

couldn't understand why they were acting so friendly, but decided it must be because their sponsor liked him.

"I guess you don't need that flying bike after all," Stu called to Alex's back. He turned around and shrugged, pretending it didn't matter to him, one way or the other.

That night Rennie and Addie came by in her father's car, and they took Alex with them to a drive-in movie. They filled up the car with popcorn, candy, and drinks, and stuck the speaker onto the open window. Outside it was warm, and the sun was just about to drop out of sight. Alex sat in the back seat while Rennie told Addie about their search.

"We went to a bunch of bike stores," he told her, "just the way your cousin told us to. I never knew there were so many around! I even went back to the Bike Exchange today, Alex, and looked at every single bike in the place. No luck."

"That was a weird place," Alex remarked. "I saw the Rainbow Toy man at the track today. He was with Rick and those guys. Can you believe it? They don't want to go pro."

"You mean they can't, they're such crazy riders," said Rennie.

"I wonder what the little man was laughing about, though," Alex said. "Remember? He kept laughing and laughing about the Rainbow Toy man and the graveyard shift. What did that mean?"

"Nothing, probably," said Rennie. "I don't even know what a graveyard shift is."

"Graveyard shift?" Addie said. "That means like working after hours, moonlighting. You know. Making extra money, sometimes on the sly. Why?"

"The guy thought it was the funniest thing he ever said in his life. The Rainbow Toy man works the graveyard shift. He went hysterical," Rennie told her. "Weird."

"And the Rainbow man was with Rick?" asked Addie. "I think *that's* weird."

She put her knees up on the dashboard and got comfortable and thoughtful at the same time. Alex leaned forward to watch and listen. A double feature of horror films was scheduled and he didn't want to admit that he could get scared by a lot of fake sneaking around and knife-throwing. He was glad he was alone in back where he could cover his eyes.

The first movie was all about graveyards. A creature made of chains was dragging around the headstones under a steel-gray moon. A crypt door flew open and banged in the wind. Clouds covered the moon and the clanking grew louder . . . Addie grabbed Rennie's hand and screamed. Alex jumped a mile.

"I've got it!" she yelled.

"What?" Rennie shouted back at her.

"The graveyard shift!"

"Tell us later."

"No, now!" she cried, and looked back at Alex who had turned very pale after her scream. "Glen Canyon is a graveyard. And you know who goes there?"

"Who?" Alex asked.

"Shh," went Rennie.

"Rick," said Addie.

"Shh," went Rennie again.

"Rick?" Alex asked.

"Shh yourself," Addie said to Rennie, letting go of his hand and putting her knees back up front.

Alex sat forward with his eyes glued to the horror on the screen. A green corpse was lifting the lid of its coffin from inside, and the chain ghost was calling *Arthur, Arthur,* while a rat scuttled out of the crypt into the grass.

"Did you say Rick?" Rennie suddenly asked.

She smiled, and let him hold her hand again.

"Yes, I did. . . . His uncle lives somewhere near Glen Canyon. That's a fancy cemetery."

"How do *you* know?" Rennie asked her.

"He used to talk about the graveyard near his uncle. How lots of people park and make out there."

"He did?" Rennie said crossly and let go of her hand. "Why would he tell you a thing like that?"

"Never mind. I never went there. I swear."

"And you never will," Rennie told her.

"It sounds like a long shot," Alex remarked, his voice expressing doubt. Actually he wanted to believe Addie's guess was the right one; he wanted to believe that Rick took the bike, and not Rennie; and of course he wanted the bike back—especially for the race in Laguna.

"But it's worth a try," Addie insisted. "He said his uncle had this gorgeous house, with a pool, right behind the graveyard."

Rennie was still mad, but he let out a big sigh and said, "Okay. We'll try Glen Canyon, Alex and me. Like I say, you're not going there."

84

"Maybe Rick took the bike," Alex said. "Wouldn't that be something?"

"I honestly doubt it," said Addie, "given the fact that he's made of money. I mean, why would he need a bike? But maybe someone he knows—you know, Stu or someone else, took it."

"It's really a wild idea," said Rennie, "but I'm willing to give it a shot."

"Great. A graveyard? After this?" Alex murmured, looking at the screen. But no one heard him.

7

That night, after the movie, Alex was too nervous to sleep. Instead he sat in bed with the light on, trying to read old comic books. But his mind kept moving around from one thought to another. He thought about Rick trying to make him feel stupid for trusting Rennie. He thought about the bike—lost!—after such a short time in his possession. He felt very strongly that he understood why Peter Pan didn't want to grow up. Everything new seemed to bring something worse along with it. He envied Robinson for being so close to the ground.

Suddenly there was a knock on his door and his father entered, looking serious. Alex was surprised, because it was so late, and his father looked as restless as Alex felt. Mr. Porter shut the door.

"We have to make a decision," he announced, and ambled around the room, examining Alex's collections of soldiers, Smurfs, comic books, and G.I. Joes. Then he added: "Actually, you have to make a decision."

"About what?" Alex asked nervously.

"Whether you want to be sponsored by a factory, or not. That man you and your mother met, from Rainbow Toys, called me at work today."

"Yag. What about?"

"He's serious about wanting to sponsor you."

"What does Mom say?"

"She made him call me, and now I'm coming to you, as the proper person to decide. We both feel you're old enough to know what having a sponsor will entail, in terms of time. And we'll both back you, however you decide." Mr. Porter stopped in front of Alex and looked down over the rims of his spectacles.

"Oh, no," Alex groaned. He lay back his head, shut his eyes, and imagined himself in a factory shirt, on a factory bike, riding all over the country. "Oh, no."

"Well, I didn't mean to make you unhappy," his father said. "At least you should be flattered. It shows you're really excellent."

Alex couldn't conceal a smile at some visions he was having: of himself, a winner, loaded with money, back on a new version of the Radical.

"The man," his father continued, "was awfully interested in the Radical . . . He wanted to know if I had already sold the design."

"Weird. Why?" Alex asked, sitting up, eyes open.

"I think he might want to buy it, or try it. I dunno. He didn't seem to understand that some things you do just for fun, and not for profit."

"If you do make another one," said Alex, "you better get a patent for it, so no one can steal the idea. . . . Will it take as long to make?"

"Well, you know me," his father said with a small smile. "It might take longer. I'm putting together design notes now. I'll patent these."

"Please, Dad. Try to rush this one," said Alex.

"What for? If you have Rainbow Toys as a sponsor, they're bound to buy you a bike to ride."

Mr. Porter then tousled Alex's hair, and told him to sleep on his decision. And after he left the room, Alex sat gazing at his trophies some more. His stomach was turning over uneasily. He went to the shelf where he had his sets of soldiers lined up, as if ready for combat. He hadn't played with them for ages, but now, for some reason, he was in the mood. He would never admit to his friends that he still liked to arrange his soldiers for battles, which he then acted out; but sometimes, when he was alone and feeling nervous, he did just that.

And the time always passed so quickly, it was as if he was dreaming. Two hours seemed like half an hour, when he heard his parents getting ready for bed, heard the lights being switched off, and his family calling goodnight from room to room. He left his soldiers in formation on the rug, yawned, and decided to sleep too.

But when he turned out his light, he couldn't sleep, but listened to the crickets outside the house. Lights from the street crossed over his shade and wall, and then he heard something scratch on his window. He thought he must be imagining it until he distinctly heard it again. It was a soft scratch on his screen.

He heard his name: "Hey, Alex!"

He went to the window and peeked out the edge of the shade.

A face looked back at him. Rennie.

Alex opened the window and whispered, "What do you want? You scared me!"

"Listen, I've got the moped for tonight. I've got to have it back early in the morning. We've got to go, now, to Glen Canyon to look for the bike."

"Now? In the night and the dark?"

Rennie nodded. "Your parents asleep?"

"I don't know. They're locked in their room. And they'd kill me if they found out."

"Alex, this is the only chance we'll get."

"Oh, okay," he said glumly.

He slipped into his jeans and shirt and edged his way through the darkened living room and out the front door. They wheeled the moped down the street so it wouldn't make noise, and took off for the freeway to Glen Canyon. Alex kept saying, "We shouldn't be doing this." He hated the way he was still suspicious of Rennie. But all the way down the freeway he kept thinking of how strange it was that Rennie wanted to do this crazy thing in the middle of the night. What was he trying to prove?

The gates of Glen Canyon cemetery were permanently open. They were black and very high, like the fence, and they had spikes on top of each pole. The fence encircled the acres of mowed grass and newly planted trees. A dark house sat at the side of the driveway, and beyond it was a stone chapel. The gravestones were pale in the moonlight. Some of them were dark, but many were cut from light marble. In the light of the moon you could see all kinds of figures: angels, lambs, crosses. But the names on the graves were hard to read.

The moped buzzed around the narrow roads that threaded through the grass, and then Rennie stopped and turned off the engine. He locked the bike beside a black pond, near the back of the cemetery. On the water, lily pads lay still.

"Why did you stop?" asked Alex, who had been straining to see the Radical as they drove.

"We have to walk, and we have to cover every inch of this place."

"But that will take hours!"

"Not if we split up," said Rennie. "That will cut the time in half."

"You're kidding, I hope. Split up?"

"Yup . . . You take that side, over there," he announced, and waved his hand at the other side of the pond. "I'll go that way." And he bravely faced the darker side of the cemetery.

"Okay now," said Rennie. "We'll meet back here at one o'clock on the dot. And let's hope one of us has the bike!"

"This is crazy," said Alex, and his mouth was very dry.

"We have to give it a try. . . . This is our last chance."

Alex scrutinized Rennie and was surprised to see some

fear in his friend's eyes. Rennie, who always seemed like the soul of confidence, the one who slept out in the wilderness alone, was now uneasy. Alex gazed across the pond and thought about Rennie's family, how poor they were and how much they needed money. He wanted to say, "Okay, Ren, did you take the bike and sell it? Just tell me and I'll forgive you."

Instead he just looked into Rennie's fear-filled eyes and pretended to be the brave one, for once.

"Okay . . . one o'clock," Alex said, and checked his watch to make sure it shone in the dark.

"Good luck," he was told.

They separated and took the roads that led in opposite directions. Alex walked slowly, trying to measure his breathing so each gulp of air calmed rather than alarmed him. Breathing deeply worked pretty well. After a while, he began to believe that it was perfectly normal to be walking around a strange graveyard in the middle of the night.

He peered behind every bush and he walked around every headstone. He carefully kept account of the names of the paths that he followed, and he cut down the middle of the cemetery, then turned back up one road over. He planned to follow the fence back to the pond. Getting lost would *not* be normal.

He almost began to enjoy the quiet and the mystery of being in such a place, though he wanted, more than anything, to find the bike. At one point he saw something silver shining on the grass, and he dodged between stones to see what it was. A grocery cart was lying on its side in the bushes. Disappointed, he walked on, but then he began to hear a strange sound, like voices murmuring and whispering.

Alex's heart pounded hard in his chest, no matter how many deep breaths he took. The fence was far away from him. He was in the middle of the cemetery, and all he could see were the black doors of stone crypts all around him. Like open holes, they stuck out of earth and stone. He hurried past them, but each one seemed to send out a cold wind from the grille in the door. And all the time he heard those voices, coming from somewhere to his right.

He didn't know whether to run toward or away from the voices. He didn't know whether to give up the search for the bike or not. He didn't know what to say to Rennie. He ran, and when he got to the fence again, he paused, listening. A faint breeze in the trees made a sound like moving cars, or water. He looked through the black leaves and realized it wasn't a forest there, but the end of a big estate. He could see a house. This made him feel a lot better, and he followed the fence to the right, hearing the voices more distinctly.

There was soft music now, as a background to the voices. Alex trailed the fence and peered through. Then he saw where the voices were coming from: there was a big white house behind some bushes. A pool, and music and some people moving around. Alex was overjoyed that they were not ghosts and that they were close by and awake while he explored. Surely they would rescue him if something awful happened.

He took a deep breath, murmured, "Whew," and went on looking for the bike. He moved faster now, as his time was running out. His hopes were running out, too; the bike became more and more of a memory, and nothing to seriously hunt for.

"This was a stupid idea in the first place," he muttered aloud.

He kicked at the ground, still looking around, but his eyes were filling with tears of disappointment.

"I'll never get another bike like that, and I'll never, ever, ever listen to Addie Sparks!"

Now he saw the pond, and Rennie was already there. No bike. He was staring at the water, looking as depressed as Alex felt.

"No luck?" he called.

"Nothing."

"You sure? Nothing?"

"The biggest thing that happened," said Alex, "was that I saw a shopping cart and I heard voices and thought there were ghosts waking up around me."

"What were they?"

"Just people. There was a big white house behind the fence, with a party going on. Music."

Rennie stared at Alex. His mouth was wide open. "What are you telling me—nothing? Don't you remember what Addie said?"

"No, what?"

"She said Rick's uncle's house was right beside this place, and it had a pool. That's why we're here. Remember?" He unlocked the moped, started the engine, and made Alex guide him to the part of the fence, where they now both saw the house.

They peered through the poles, and saw a gathering of people, mostly males, and heard Frank Sinatra crooning in the background.

"Come on, let's go check this out," Rennie whispered.

"What do you mean?"

"We'll go around to the front of that place and see if it belongs to Rick's uncle."

"No way, Rennie. I want to go home. We'd never be able to tell if it belongs to his uncle anyway."

"You have no faith, man. You give up too fast."

They stared at each other angrily.

"And why are you being so pushy about this idea of Rick taking the bike? Why would he need it? He's rich. He's got a bike."

"I just figure we should check it out, that's all. . . . Come on. We'll just look at the front of the house. Then we'll go home."

Alex shrugged and gave up, and Rennie spun them out of the cemetery. They wound around a few side streets, until they figured they were on the road that bordered the back of the cemetery. Alex was yawning and restless as they passed huge hedges and trees which hid the houses. They buzzed along slowly until they spotted the top of a big white house. Then Rennie insisted on riding all the way up the driveway to make sure it was the right place.

It was. The same music was pouring from inside, and they could hear the splashes of people in the pool.

"Still," said Alex, "this doesn't mean it's the uncle's house."

"I know, I know."

Cars were parked near the entrance and Rennie sat still, surveying the property and the front of the house, as if he was going to buy it. Alex stared, instead, at a black truck parked there. Its license was BMX RCR. He clutched Rennie's back.

"Let's go, Ren, come on," he said.

"Okay, man, relax. I'd sure like to look in that garage, though—just to check, you know."

"No! Go!"

"Okay, okay, I'm going."

They swerved back down the driveway. Alex's eyes were blazing, as if he had just looked directly into the sun.

"Rennie," he shouted. "For some reason, I think that *was* the uncle's place."

"Yeah? Why?" Rennie called back.

"I can't explain it. I just do."

He squinted into the wind and kept his mouth shut tight. He didn't want to tell Rennie about the truck—not yet. His mind was speeding now, around the facts. The sponsor was there, in that exact house; but why? Did Rennie know where to look? Did he know the sponsor? All he could visualize were the beef-red face and the gold chain, and the image gave him the creeps. If the sponsor was not connected with Addie's story about Rick, then what coincidence could put him there in that house at that exact hour?

"I think it was the right place, too," Rennie called to him.

"So what will we do next?"

"I'll figure something out," Rennie said with assurance. "Don't worry."

"Don't worry?" Alex thought. "You've got to be kidding."

8

"It was just a coincidence, after all."

These were Alex's last words to himself that night, before he fell asleep. But all night he dreamed of the letters BMX RCR as the parts of a code he must crack. In real life, the letters obviously meant Bicycle Motor Cross Racer. In Alex's dream life they came to mean Big Meat Cracking Robber. He had visions of the beefy sponsor taking him to a track where hundreds of stolen bikes glittered in a golden pot and he was told to find his bike as fast as he could. It was a nightmare; he couldn't find it. No matter how hard he pulled at the spokes and handlebars in the piles of bikes, none of them would move.

When he woke up and fumbled his way into the bright light of the living room, his mother was there.

"It's eleven o'clock, Alex," she announced. "You went to bed at ten. Let me feel your head. I'm sure you're sick."

"I'm fine, Mom, really," Alex protested. "I just had a bad dream." She would have a fit if he told her he came in after two in the morning.

She put her hand on his forehead. "I guess you are," she agreed, but looked puzzled.

He really wanted to tell her all that had happened, and to get her opinion on the situation. He wanted to ask if she thought it was all a coincidence? Instead, he just told her he had a nightmare, and he went and played a game on the Colecovision with Rosie.

"Alex," his mother said, "we have to run out later on. The barbecue. So will you babysit?"

"Sure, okay," he muttered absently, he was so involved in a game of Venture.

"During your bad dream, did you make up your mind about a sponsorship?" she asked.

"Sponsorship?" He felt a flash, like an electric current under his skin. "Uh-oh—no. I haven't decided, but I think maybe I'll wait."

"Wait? For what?"

"Maybe somebody else will offer it to me," he told her.

"You don't like that Rainbow man?"

"Rainbow man," he said, bewildered. "I think of him as Beef man," he told her. "Rainbow man . . . ?"

"Shh," went Rosie. "Whenever it's my turn, you talk."

100

"Okay, okay," he said, and his face slowly took on light as he realized that the bikes in his dream were lying in the pot of gold at the end of a rainbow. "Rainbow man . . . pot of gold. It's not a coincidence, at least in the dream," he whispered to himself.

"Well, it's up to you," his mother continued. "I mean, if you want to wait, it's really up to you."

Alex looked up at her. Whenever she used those words, it meant she thought he was making a mistake, being too timid.

"It's really up to you, but have you thought about next weekend's race? If we go, you can bring your old GT, and probably still find a sponsor. You know, it's the big race. We don't want to miss it."

"I don't want to go without the Radical," he told her. "You can go with Robinson and Rosie. But I don't want to."

"Alex," she said with a tone of disapproval. "I'm sick about you losing that bike, too. But don't get so down so fast."

"Just give me some time to decide," he said, and pretended to focus on Rosie's game while his mind was actually lost in last night's adventure and last night's nightmare, both of which added up to the same thing.

After lunch Rennie and Addie arrived with her little brother, Moses. Alex had been waiting impatiently all morning to talk to Rennie, and now he was annoyed by the presence of the others.

Addie said, with her dimpled smile, "Oh! I guess you're

stuck babysitting like me, Alex . . . Moses, look at that pool!"

"Can he go for a dip, Alex?" said Rennie. "That's what she's really trying to say."

"Can he swim?"

"I brought his water wings."

"Okay, sure," Alex agreed.

Moses was a small boy, who looked like a robot with glasses. He and Robinson stood staring at each other, as if they were looking in a mirror and didn't like what they saw. Both let their mouths hang open, and their eyes stopped blinking. They just stared.

"Why don't you swim with him, Rob?" Alex suggested, trying not to laugh.

"Come here," said Robinson, and pulled Alex across the room. "Don't you know he's one of my emenies? Why is he here?"

"To swim, dummy. Don't be selfish."

"I'm not swimming with him."

"No one said you are. Just watch him."

Addie helped Moses out of his clothes. He was wearing Smurf trunks under his jeans.

"Addie wants to swim too," said Rennie, "but she's too shy to say so."

"Go ahead," Alex told her, and they all went out to the pool's edge. They watched Moses hand over his glasses, stick his arms into his water wings, and slowly ease himself into the blue water. He was serious and silent all that time. Robinson was too. He stood and stared.

Addie went inside to change, and the little boy plunged

into the water and began to paddle around with his head stuck up like a turtle, his mouth sealed tight, and his eyes blinking off drops of water. You could tell he wanted to smile, but wasn't allowing himself that pleasure.

"I'll turn on some music," Alex announced.

He went inside and turned on the radio, so the outdoor speakers opened onto the garden and the pool. Then Robinson went into his room and changed into his trunks and water wings, and Addie came out in a black bikini and dived in.

"Where's Rosie?" asked Rennie.

"At a friend's."

"So you're stuck here for the day?"

"Yeah," Alex sighed, then his expression changed and he looked at his friend with some suspicion. "Why are you asking? I can tell you have some plan in mind."

"Well, man, see, I've got Addie's father's car. And I think we'll go back to Glen Canyon, her and me, just to look around some more."

"I don't know, Rennie. It could be dangerous, really dangerous."

"Oh, don't believe that. I think we're getting warm. The bike is somewhere around there."

They stood and watched Addie do clean strokes up and down the length of the pool, while Robinson did the cannonball jump into the water, obviously showing off to Moses, who got splashed. Then the two little boys, with their orange water wings bobbing beside them, stared at each other some more.

"Could Moses stay here for an hour or so while

Addie and I go and explore?" asked Rennie.

"Why not leave Addie here and bring me?"

"It's her father's car, man, and she wants to come . . . She's a little crazy," he said with a grin.

"Just don't take too long," Alex told him. He didn't relish the idea of babysitting two boys who considered themselves "emenies," while Rennie went off to look for a bike he might have stolen himself. But he was glad that they hadn't given up on Glen Canyon.

He watched Rennie call Addie out of the water, and wondered how to tell him about the black truck. He didn't want to sound foolish, and a small part of him even doubted that he really had seen the license BMX   RCR. Maybe he had seen a license which almost said that.

"Rennie," he called, "if you go up that driveway again—"

"I'm planning to."

"—look and see what the license on the black truck is . . . if it's still there," Alex suggested.

"I remember what it was," said Rennie.

"You do? Why?"

"Because I'm a genius."

"Then what was it?" asked Alex with a suspicious squint in his eyes.

"BMX   RCR . . . You think I'm an idiot or something? That license is what caught my eye. That's why I think we're almost there."

Alex bit his bottom lip and tried to look cool and stupid at the same time. "Oh, yeah, I get it," he said, "I guess you're right."

104

Then Addie ran by them in her wet suit and Rennie
threw a towel at her. The two little boys floated in the
pool together, staring up.

After Rennie and Addie had left, Alex made Moses and
Robinson leave the pool and come inside. Moses stuck on
his glasses and sat with his arms folded, all dressed again,
in Mr. Porter's big armchair. Robinson went to get some
Lego and sat on the floor, where Moses could see him;
and he wondered what to build.

He talked to himself while he moved the parts of the
Lego around.

"I once made a castle so big I could put Alex's soldiers
in it, and we had a war, and then I took it apart to make
a garage, but I wish I could make a castle again . . . and
play with Alex's soldiers."

"Why can't you?" Moses asked, and looked as if his
own voice had surprised him.

Robinson replied, "It takes too long, and besides, Alex
is very, very selfish."

"Let's build the castle anyway," Moses suggested.

"Mm, okay," Robinson muttered.

Moses slipped out of the chair and smiled for the first
time since his arrival. It was a big smile and gave him
dimples like his sister's. Robinson smiled back, and Alex
told them he could use some of his soldiers, if they were
careful. Now he could relax and forget about them. He
watched television while they played, and made them all
a big bowl of popcorn. But he kept going to the window
to look out for Rennie and Addie. His mother said she'd

be home around four, and Rennie promised he'd be back before three-thirty.

However, when at three Rennie had still not returned, Alex began to feel sick to his stomach, he was so nervous. He hardly dared to imagine that they might return with the bike, but he couldn't help it. Waiting was no fun at all. He realized he would much rather be taking his chances at the strange house than sitting at home, imagining the worst.

The two little boys were lost in the Lego castle and the soldiers, when Alex heard the rumble of the car's engine. He rushed outside.

Addie was alone.

"Where's Ren?" asked Alex.

She just sat there, breathing hard, with the engine still running. Her face looked very white, and her hair very copper. He peered in the open window and repeated his question.

"God, Alex," was all she said, "I can't believe I made it. I only have a trainer's license. If my father knew! If the police—! Oh, God, what an experience!"

"Yeah, but where's Rennie?"

She switched off the engine and leaned back her head, and her lips quivered. "He's back there," she whispered. "Somewhere . . . Alex, he just disappeared!"

"You mean you left him at the house?"

"Get in the car, quick. I'll tell you everything."

Alex jumped in beside her. "Go on. Tell!"

"Okay. We got there, right? No problem. We parked outside the white house. On the street. It was real quiet," she whispered, "and it looked like no one was there. We walked up the driveway. Rennie said he wanted to look in the garage. But it's one of those electronic jobs you need a thing for—to open, you know?"

"Yeah, yeah, I know," Alex said, hurrying her.

"There were no cars, and the house looked dark . . . I snuck around the side, by the bushes, to check. I could see light in the back. Rennie was trying, meanwhile, to get into the garage, through a side door. I looked in one of the downstairs windows, right beside me. The room was empty. A real fancy dining room. And I saw a man through the doors, in another room, a kind of den. At a desk . . . I saw him take a gun out of his drawer. He got up. He was big! He started toward the front of the house . . . I was so scared! I hid in the bushes, praying that Rennie would come to join me. But he didn't. I waited and waited. Then I heard a banging noise, and I ran about ninety miles an hour back to the car. I waited there for about half an hour. Then I snuck back to the garage area. No Rennie . . . I hung around for an hour and a half."

"Did you look in the window again?" Alex asked, with his heart pounding.

"Yes, and I didn't see anyone!"

"Help," said Alex.

"I know," she agreed. "I'm so scared!"

"Was it a—was it—was it a gunshot?"

"The bang? I don't know! I never heard a gun before." She was almost crying, and Alex was embarrassed. "I had to leave. My father will kill me if he finds out I'm driving."

"Okay, okay, you better go. . . . But Addie. What

do you think happened? Where's Rennie?"

"I think they've got him in that house. I really do," she said.

"Do you think we should tell my parents?"

"I'd rather figure it out without any grownups."

"So would I. But what if something bad has happened to Rennie? The police will have to be notified," Alex said, making a big effort at being calm.

A tear rolled down Addie's cheek. "I feel so guilty," she said. "I shouldn't have left him there. But I had to!"

"Don't worry. You know Rennie. He'll find his way out," Alex said.

"If he can," she added.

Then Alex went inside and got Moses for Addie to bring home. The two little boys were not happy, now, to say good-bye. Robinson made Moses promise to come back soon and finish working on the Lego castle with him. And after Moses was gone, Robinson fussed around Alex, talking nonstop, until Alex turned on the television at full volume. He sat there, with his hands over his ears, imagining every terrifying detail Addie told him: the huge house, the bushes, the empty dining room and the den where the man sat, the gun in his hand, and Rennie fumbling around the garage. He could imagine a man jump out and grab Rennie by the hair or neck, and haul him inside. He could see the man threaten Rennie.

"Alex!" Robinson screamed, and turned the sound off the television. *"Listen to me!"*

"What do you want now?" Alex asked him.

"Mommy and Daddy just drove in . . . You can stop babysitting now."

"Whew! I'm glad to hear that," Alex told him, and he walked out of the room, aiming to escape. All he wanted was to get on his bike, and go—where he didn't know. But he had this burning feeling in his head, as if his hair was on fire. He had to help Rennie, and make up for all the bad thoughts he had been having toward his friend. He knew now that Rennie had not stolen the bike, and his guilt was overwhelming.

"Be right back," he called to his mother, and rode away.

The first place he went was to the adobe house down near the freeway. The air was misty from smog and the rush-hour traffic was tailing its way along the nearby freeway away from the larger cities. When he knocked on the door of Rennie's house and waited impatiently for a response, Alex felt as if he hadn't slept for nights.

After a few minutes, Rennie's father appeared, and he didn't look well at all. His brown face had a gray tone to it, and he had big dark circles under his eyes. Still, he tried to smile at Alex.

"You looking for my boy again?" he asked.

"Yes, I just wondered—"

"I'm looking for him, too. Can you tell him that when you see him?"

"Oh sure," Alex said at once.

"Tell him I'm not too well, and might have to go to the hospital. Tell him to be home tonight. Okay?"

"Sure," Alex said again, and gulped. "I'll tell him."

Rennie's father thanked him, and Alex mounted the bike and rode home at top speed. When he got there, he dragged the telephone into his bedroom and called Addie.

"Anything?" he asked her.

"Nothing," she said. "What'll we do?"

"I'm not going to tell my parents yet," he told her. "First I'm going to ride to Glen Canyon myself and see what I can find."

"Alex! Are you sure you should do that?"

"No," he confessed. "But I'm going to, anyway."

"Call me the minute you get back. I'm grounded for driving alone."

In the kitchen, Alex told his mother he was going for a long bike trip on his father's ten-speed. "Just for fun," he explained.

"In this heat? It's already five!"

"Oh well. It's better than sitting around."

She eyed him as if she suspected he wasn't telling the whole truth.

"You want to bring a snack with you?" she asked.

"That's not a bad idea," he admitted.

She watched him slap together a peanut-butter-and-jelly sandwich, and then she dropped a cold Coke into his sandwich bag.

"Robinson said he had a friend over today," she remarked.

"Yeah. Addie's little brother."

"Where was Addie?"

"Uh, she and Rennie wanted to be alone. I mean, they just went to the hills or something. I don't know."

"Robinson said they went to Glen Canyon. What for? Is the cemetery the new place to park, or something?"

"Mom! How would I know?" said Alex, and imagined himself breaking Robinson's Lego castle with one kick.

"Well, be careful biking," she concluded.

"Don't worry."

"And be back before dark."

"If I'm not, you can call the police," said Alex.

"You look kind of ragged around the edges, Alex. Tired again?"

"Robinson drove me crazy all afternoon. That's all," he said, and he swept up his sandwich and banged out of the house.

He hated the way mothers always suspect you of doing something bad. Especially his mother. She just couldn't trust him, he thought to himself, and then he remembered how he had been suspicious of Rennie. And he felt guilty and stupid all over again. He mounted his father's ten-speed bike and headed for the foothill road, instead of the freeway. He had never felt so independent before. He followed a pretty direct and shady route to Glen Canyon. The heat was his only problem, besides the fact that he didn't know what he was going to do when he got there. But he liked the feeling of confidence he had, even though the circumstances for it were not exactly fun. He realized that he felt older than he ever had before. The sense of age was a shock; he didn't know what had happened to bring it on, or when exactly he had begun to change.

9

The house looked bigger and more solid in the light of day. Alex stood at the end of the drive, staring up at the white two-story house and windows. He imagined Rennie inside one of the rooms, where white curtains hung like screens across the glass. He imagined him tied to a bedpost with a cloth wrapped around his head and through his teeth.

"I wish this would be easy!" Alex sighed under his breath. He locked his bike around a tree, pocketed the key, and walked up the driveway, not even knowing what he was going to do. He was letting some instinct lead him. There was nothing else to do. He went directly to the door beside the garage and rang the bell. He assumed it led into a kitchen or pantry.

A woman, who looked like she might act on *The Love Boat,* answered. She was wearing pink shorts, no shoes, a purple halter top and a bridge of white cream across her nose. Her eyes were hidden by large red sunglasses which clashed with everything else she wore. To Alex she looked like a person who hated kids.

"Yes," she drawled, in a bored voice.

"Uh, um, uh, I've lost something," Alex announced.

"Is that so . . . What?"

"Well, I mean, um, could I look around?"

"What did you lose?" she asked.

"A kitten. . . . It ran away from our house. Up the street. I'm visiting some people up the street, see, and we brought a litter of kittens with us. And this one disappeared."

"Yeah? That's too bad . . . Go ahead," she said, and shut the door in his face.

"Talk about genius," Alex said to himself, and smiled.

He walked around the front of the garage. There were no windows on the large electronic door, but he vaguely remembered a window on the side. He slipped around the house, calling, "Here, kitty, kitty, kitty!" And when he came to the window, he peered in and saw a gray Impala parked there, along with about twelve BMX bikes. They were lined up along a far wall. Alex held his hands up around his eyes and passed his face close to the glass. Most of the bikes were Red Lines and a couple of GTs were there, too. And stuck behind all of them stood a bike which looked to him a lot like the Radical.

He pressed his thumbs under the window sash and started to push up, but then he didn't dare. Not yet. Instead he decided to hunt for Rennie, and pushed through bushes, toward the back of the house, loudly calling, "Here, kitty, kitty, kitty!"

He found himself near the pool, and saw the same lady sitting out there in a lounge chair. She was alone. She turned and stared at him, while she revolved gum around between her teeth.

"No luck?" she asked.

He shook his head.

"What color is the kitten?"

"Yellow. Like marmalade," he told her.

"And its name?"

Alex looked at the bright blue pool water flashing under the sun and tried not to smile when he said, "Sparky."

"That's the cutest name. . . . Go ahead. Call over by the fence there," she said in a friendly voice, and pointed toward the back of the yard. "Maybe it strayed into the cemetery. Then you'll never find it. Yuck. I hate having that place right there. Spook city!"

Alex did as she said and called the kitten from the other side of the pool. He realized she was the type of woman who didn't hate kids after all. She was more the type who liked to talk a whole lot, and he figured she was his best bet on getting information. He came back to where she sat and made a very sad face.

"My little brother will cry and cry if I don't find it," he said.

"Maybe it went up a tree. You know, sometimes they do that when they're scared." She yawned then and leaned back her head. "This is my day off, honey, so I won't help you, if you don't mind. I'm a beautician. On my feet all day."

"Oh, that's okay."

"My husband will be home soon. He's a sucker for kids and animals. So you can bet on his help."

"Why does he have all those bikes in the garage. Do you have a lot of kids?" asked Alex.

"Nah. Not yet. Those belong to his brother, Paul, who works for a company. Toys. He's a salesman, but then he acts as a sponsor, whatever that means, for BMX. You like BMX?"

"Yup," Alex muttered, but his mind was way off somewhere, fitting pieces of the puzzle together. It wasn't hard. Things were falling into place, and he wasn't sure he liked it.

"Well, listen, come here," she whispered, and signaled for him to lean down. "So does this Mexican kid who's inside the house."

"Really? What do you mean?" asked Alex, and he kneeled down on the ground beside her. His eyes scanned the windows on the back of the house.

"You've got a brother, right?" she asked, and Alex nodded. "Well, then you should know how it is. These two guys, my husband and his brother, they can't agree on anything. Never could."

"And they're fighting now?"

"Over the boy. He was trespassing—breaking and entering, to be exact—and my husband caught him," she whispered. "Now, that would have been that, except for Paul interfering."

"Wow. How?"

"I don't know," she admitted, "not exactly. All I know is my Joe is a decent guy, and he wanted to let the kid go. Felt sorry for him. But not Paul. Paul has plans. I don't know what they are."

"Awesome," murmured Alex.

"Want to know a secret?"

"Sure, what?"

"I don't like Paul."

Alex was longing to say, "I don't either," but instead he tried to figure out a way to get more information. "Maybe Paul is going to turn him over to the police?" he suggested.

"If he was going to do that, he would've done it right away. That's what I don't get. Meantime my Joe has driven all the way to Taco Bell to get the kid some food."

"He sounds really nice," Alex said.

"Yeah, but I hope they get it settled. Soon. I can't stand a mess of any kind."

"Well, I'll go on calling the kitten," Alex told her, sensing she was finished with her story.

He wandered away from the poolside to the other side of the house, and now he called, "Kitty, kitty, kitty" even louder, hoping that Rennie would hear his voice. His mind was racing. What should he do to get Rennie out of there? It was a big relief to know he was alive and well and being fed by Taco Bell; but Paul's presence ruined all those facts.

Alex couldn't even imagine what plans the man had for Rennie.

He saw an open window and looked through it into the kitchen, which was shiny and clean. He put his face up to the screen and called, "Kitty, kitty, Rennie, kitty, kitty, Rennie!"

Then he heard the crunch of a car coming up the graveled driveway, and jumped back flat against the house. He peered around a bush, and saw it wasn't a car, after all. It was a truck—*the* truck—license plate: BMX RCR. And at the wheel was the beefy sponsor, Paul: with him were two other men whom Alex couldn't see that well. He stayed where he was beside the kitchen window, and took one more chance at calling. He heard the garage door open up.

"Kitty, kitty, Rennie, kitty, kitty, Rennie!"

Then he stepped back from the window again. The men were slamming out of the truck and speaking in angry voices, which almost drowned out the voice beside Alex.

It said: "Wow, man. You're a genius!"

Alex jumped out of his skin, then grinned and whispered at Rennie's face on the other side of the screen, "Quick, stupid. Climb out!"

Both of them pushed at the screen and jogged it up, so Rennie could squeeze out and jump onto the ground beside Alex. Both were beaming and grabbing each other's arms, they were so glad to see each other.

"I gotta get the Radical, man. It's in the garage," said Rennie. "What are you riding?"

"My dad's bike."

118

"Go for it, then. Ride like hell. I'll meet you at the entrance to the cemetery. We can hide there. . . . Quick!"

The moment the men were inside the house, the two boys took off on their heels, sprinting. Alex shot down the driveway and didn't look back. However, his hands were shaking and he couldn't unlock the bike. He shook and trembled and messed it up, until finally it snapped open, just as Rennie whirled down the drive on the Radical.

"My bike!" Alex cried.

"Don't look at it now," Rennie called, "and don't look back. Ride for your life! They know I've escaped."

They pedaled, Alex in the lead, top speed around the neighborhood streets and into Glen Canyon cemetery. Alex headed for the pond, with Rennie beside him, until they stopped in the shadow of a stone angel. There they collapsed, breathless.

"Tell—tell me—everything," Alex gasped.

"I will, I will. Just let me catch my wind. Wait . . ."

For a couple of minutes he lay flat on his back on the grass, his eyes shut, his breathing fast. Alex's gaze meantime was fixed securely on the Radical where it lay gleaming in the sun. He reached out his hand to touch it, as if touching is believing, not seeing.

"Oh, wow," sighed Rennie, "I was looking forward to an enchilada. I'm starving!"

"Later, Ren. First tell me what happened," Alex insisted.

Then a tingle went down his spine. He saw the black truck slowly cruising up the other side of the pond.

119

"Oh no!" he cried. "Look who's coming!"

"Let's go," Rennie ordered.

They then mounted the bikes again and aimed for the main gates at high speed. The truck began to pursue them, speeding between the gravestones, down the narrow roads, turning up dust and screeching around the curves. The two boys tore out of Glen Canyon and up a side street, with Rennie now in the lead on the Radical. Alex thought he must be asleep, having a nightmare, as he heard the truck burning rubber behind them. It came close to Alex, as if for a sideswipe, and he swerved, hit a pole, and fell. The truck went on after Rennie, who grazed the curb and fell, too.

Alex, watching all the time, jumped up and began to push his bike in their direction. He saw Rennie struggling to hold onto the Radical, and the big beefy man pulling at the handlebars and shouting. It was impossible to hear what he said, because Rennie was yelling how he'd get the police if the man didn't leave him alone.

Alex zoomed up on his bike and banged against the beefy man's legs, but he seemed to be made of steel. He didn't flinch. Instead he tore the Radical out of Rennie's grip and hurled it into the back of the truck in one move.

"Come on, give me yours," he said to Alex. "Nothing to fear."

"You've got to be kidding!" Alex shouted.

And he and Rennie clung to the ten-speed, while the man pulled and jerked at it. Finally, he got it away and threw it back on top of the Radical. Alex wanted to cry, and saw that Rennie did, too.

120

"Okay, boys, get in," the man commanded like a general. Then he looked in their faces and suddenly his tone changed. His voice became as smooth as ice cream. "Hey now, this is really ridiculous. I just want to talk to you boys and straighten out our misunderstanding."

"We better do what he says," Rennie told Alex.

"Are you serious?"

"Listen to your pal," the sponsor said sweetly. "Hop in."

"In back," said Alex, "and not in front with you."

"Okay, okay, but come on."

Alex and Rennie climbed in with their bikes and sat huddled in the back, while the truck lurched forward and drove too fast down the suburban streets.

"Tell me what's going on, please," Alex said.

"I'm not sure, but they're probably not going to hurt us. The other guy is nice."

"I know all that," said Alex impatiently. "But what's going on?"

"The way I figure it, this creep has had your bike inspected, so he can sell the idea to his company. That's why he took it."

"But all that is against the law!" said Alex.

"I know, but I'm pretty sure that's it. I heard him talking to his brother. The brother was really mad at him. He said something about this man keeping the bike for illegal reasons."

"They why does he want us now? Why are we going back to the house?"

"That I don't know," said Rennie, his eyes wide with

alarm that he couldn't hide. He dropped his head down on his arms and told Alex how he had been locked in a bedroom by Paul, while the two brothers quarreled. He admitted he had been really scared. "And I still am," he concluded.

Alex watched as they pulled up the driveway again; his heart was pumping extra hard. The truck stopped abruptly, and the man jumped out and came to the back.

"Okay, boys, you've proved yourselves," he said. "You've got your bike back . . . right? Well, now, Alex, I know you come from a decent family, and they'll be worried if you aren't home on time. So you can relax. I'll have you back in no time. Climb out."

"And what about Rennie? He's coming home with me," said Alex.

"Sure. You think I want to keep him around?"

The two boys climbed out of the truck and followed him to the door, where he stopped and faced them.

"The point is, I'll be taking both of you home soon, but I want to come to an understanding first."

"What do you mean," said Rennie suspiciously.

"Here's how it goes. My nephew, Rick—you know him— he's in the house right now."

"Rick?" asked Alex wonderingly.

"Yeah, you know him and he knows you, and he also knows a girl named Addie Sparks." At this point the sponsor gave Rennie a long dirty look. "He likes her and he pulled this stunt, as you boys will do, and took that beautiful bike back there. Your bike, Alex. He thought it belonged to the Mexican."

"Is that so," said Rennie in a low, angry voice.

"Rick was going to give it back, natch."

"Sure," said Alex.

"He threw it in the back of my truck, at the track. I didn't know it was there until I got home. . . . Then I gave the kid hell."

"Hey, but why didn't you say anything to me?" Alex asked. "Why did you hang onto it for so long?"

The guy's face reddened a little and he still barred the door as he said, "You want to know why? I thought Rick ought to tell you himself. That's why. It was his problem, not mine."

"It seemed like *my* problem, not Rick's," Alex muttered.

"Now what do you want us to understand?" asked Rennie.

"That it was all a big mix-up, no harm intended. And I hope you won't need to tell your folks about it, Alex . . . I mean, if the Mexican hadn't broken the law today, you would've had your bike back anyway. On the front porch of your house. But he insisted on breaking and entering. Which carries some pretty heavy charges . . . if you get my meaning."

The boys looked at each other with full understanding of what the man meant. He would press charges, criminal charges, against Rennie, if the boys told their parents what had happened.

"Come on inside now," the sponsor said. "And think it over."

The house was cool and dimly lit. The carpet felt as if it were a foot deep. Alex's feet sank down into the softness, while his stomach felt like jelly. He wished he could have two minutes alone with Rennie, but all they could do was make faces at each other. One looked as scared as the other. On their right was a large dining room, all fixed up with chandeliers, and a cabinet filled with expensive glasses and plates. On their left was the den, where Addie must have looked and seen the man pull out the gun. Through a window at the end of the hall, Alex saw the woman by the pool, still lounging with her face and her feet up.

In the den was Rick, seated on a black leather couch. His face was red, as were his eyes.

"Okay, Rick," said the sponsor, "the ball is in your court now. Speak." And he stayed behind Rennie and Alex, in the doorway, like a huge prison warden.

"I'm sorry, Alex, I really am," said Rick in a soft voice. "I thought the bike belonged to Rennie—"

"So what? You stole it," Alex said.

"I was going to give it back. I really was."

"How do we know that?"

"If he hadn't come snooping around," he said with a mean look at Rennie, "I would have gotten it back to you . . . today!"

Then everyone was silent, waiting to see if Rick was going to cry or not. He looked as if he was.

"I'll pay you if you don't tell anyone," Rick said finally in a muffled voice.

"Pay who?" asked Alex.

"You."

124

"Forget it."

"My uncles have already punished me. And they told my dad. And now he's grounded me for the whole summer," he said with a sob.

Alex, embarrassed, glanced at Rennie for help. Rennie raised his eyebrows and shrugged.

"Let's get out of here and forget all of it," he said.

The sponsor said, "Way to go, kid, way to go . . . Come on, now, Rick, blow your nose and get up. They're not going to talk, and neither are we."

Rick found tissues in a desk drawer, blew his nose, and followed them all out of the house to the truck.

"We'll sit in back with our bikes," Alex said, and he looked at the sponsor and Rick as if they didn't smell very good.

He and Rennie sat in the back, leaning on the Radical and the ten-speed as if they were soft and comfortable. As the truck headed out to the freeway, they both agreed not to speak about anything that had happened until they were safe at home. Meantime, they didn't notice Rick watching them through the rearview mirror, with an expression that said, "I'll get you back for this."

It was nearly dark when they were dropped off at the corner of Alex's street, out of sight of his house. They rode home on the bikes in triumph. But no one was around, so they went for a swim. They propped the Radical out by the pool and kept it in sight, whatever they did. Alex kept looking at it with disbelief.

"I can't wait to show Dad, I just can't wait!" he kept saying.

Rennie first called his father and promised to be home that same night, and then he called Addie, who insisted on sneaking over with Moses. Her parents had grounded her, but they were the types who didn't pay attention to their own rules.

"There's a National next weekend," Alex realized, "and I'm not going to miss it. Not with the Radical back."

"Practice tomorrow? I'll come watch you before or after work," said Rennie.

"Great," said Alex from where he was perched on the bike's seat at the edge of the pool.

Finally they heard the sound of Mr. Porter's and Rosie's voices, followed by Robinson's and his mother's. They were all carrying bags of groceries into the kitchen. Mr. Porter was explaining inflation to Rosie, using a can of tuna fish as an example. Rosie peered out at the pool, and Alex watched her face change from halfhearted curiosity to disbelief. She turned and grabbed her father's hand and pulled him outside. Alex pushed the Radical into full view, beaming. His father stopped in his tracks, while his face lit up in an expression of amazement. Then he shouted for his wife and Robinson to come outside. They did, as if they were on fire, screaming, jumping for joy. Only Rosie was calm, saying, over and over again, "I really don't believe this."

"Tell us what happened. Quick!" Mariel cried.

"Soon," said Alex. "Wait."

"For what?" asked Mr. Porter.

"For Addie and Moses."

Alex insisted he wanted everyone who mattered to be

there when he told the story of how the bike was found. He made everyone line up along the edge of the pool, and when Addie and Moses were finally there, he perched on the end of the diving board and described the whole adventure.

While he was talking, he could see his father getting more and more restless, moving up and down the edge of the pool and fiddling with the net, running it across the top of the water, in search of fallen insects or leaves. Finally, when Alex finished, Mr. Porter threw down the net, lifted his hand up to his eyes like a visor, and shouted: "That man is an out-and-out criminal!"

Everyone turned to stare at him. Even the breeze seemed to fall still, as only the pool gurgled in the background.

"I bet you anything he copied my design for the bike. And what's more, I bet he plans to sell it, if he hasn't already."

"That big ugly bum," Alex's mother called out. "Come on. Let's go get him, right now. Come on. We'll bring the police along."

"And to top it all off, he almost killed Rennie and Alex, chasing them around in that truck," Mr. Porter continued, in a lower voice now. "It's unbelievable that someone like that is walking around, and selling toys, too. Rainbow Toys, my eye. It should be called Nightmare toys, instead."

"But, Dad," Alex called out. "I don't get it. Rick stole the bike, not his uncle."

"If that was the case, then why did the uncle let the bike stay there so long?" Mr. Porter asked. "And why did he keep Rennie locked up like that?"

"Rennie," asked Alex's mother, "what did he say to you? Why did he keep you there?"

Rennie, pressed between Moses and Robinson, looked perplexed. "He and his brother, I guess, put me in the room, instead of turning me over to the cops. I guess they wanted to hold me there while they went to get Rick."

"But did they threaten you?" asked Mr. Porter.

"They just said I'd be in worse trouble if I tried to escape."

Moses looked up at Rennie and squinted. "Were you scared?" he asked.

"Sure, I was," Rennie admitted at once. "But I was partly scared because I shouldn't have broken in, in the first place. I committed a crime, let's face it. They could've handed me over to the cops."

"Well, frankly, I know who *I* think committed a crime, and it isn't you," said Alex's mother.

"No. It *isn't* you," Alex agreed.

Mr. Porter resumed his restless activity of running the net across the surface of the pool. His face had settled into its usual serious and abstracted expression. He looked as if he was seeing way beyond the light of the moon, even as he looked at the water.

His wife rattled the car keys, and said, "Come on. Let's go get that big ugly man."

"No, dear," Mr. Porter murmured. "Not tonight. I want to sleep on it. You know I don't like to act too hastily."

She lifted her eyes up to the sky and nodded her head. "Do I ever know it," she agreed.

128

And all the others around the pool nodded in unison at her words. But soon they were blasting music out onto the patio. Moses and Robinson were racing each other with their orange water wings bouncing up and down on the water, while Rennie, Rosie and Addie played a game of poker using tortilla chips for chips. Alex stood next to his bike and watched everyone having a good time. He felt more like his father than he had ever felt before; that is, he felt cautious. For some reason, he was not ready to celebrate yet.

10

The next morning, Alex rode, with Robinson and his mother, to the local track to practice. They were all in a good mood, and Mrs. Porter even went so far as to listen to country-western music. She sang loudly, "Thank God, I'm a Country Boy," embarrassing Alex.

"Mom, please don't sing after we've picked up my friends," Alex said, trying to sound polite about it.

"You're so stuffy, Alex. You're like a little old man," she retorted.

Robinson thought that was very funny and grinned up at his brother, who sat beside him in the front seat.

Halfway to Meridian, they stopped to pick up a couple

of Alex's friends and their bikes, and soon they were all at the track with lunches packed and plans to stay until four.

"I'll pick you guys up then," Mrs. Porter said. "And be sure you take good care of Robinson. . . . And please say a little prayer for your dad and me."

"Don't worry," Alex told her. He was sitting on the Radical, lifting and dropping the front wheel, eager to move. He really didn't want to think about his mother and father confronting the Rainbow man.

"If you have any problems, use the pay phone down the road."

"Oh come on, Mom, we'll be fine!"

She jumped up into the truck, turned on the radio and began to sing out the window, at the top of her lungs, so all Alex's friends could hear her. Then she drove off in a cloud of dust.

Robinson tried to hide the smile on his lips and followed the bigger boys to the track. The sun was beating down on the dust. There were a few other kids already there, practicing jumps and starts. Alex and Robinson were the only ones wearing helmets, and they were a little embarrassed by that. But they had promised their mother they would.

Alex put on his racing gloves and pushed the Radical up the hill to the starting gate. It was lying flat down and the track had not been watered, so it was rough. But when he was off and pedaling, he had speed beyond belief, and a ride so smooth, it was as if he rode inches off the ground. He did wheelies feet into the air, at the crest of each jump, while the other riders stopped and stared with envy.

While he was making each ride look like a stunt event, he was thinking about how much fun this was, more fun than racing, even. The bike would hardly let him ride normally, even when he tried. And he did try, just to see what would happen. He tried to go at a regular pace down the starting hill and around the berms and over the whoop-de-dos. But the bike zoomed under his hands into a lightning-speed effect. Its weight was feathery, something he could hardly control. He tried to limit his wheelies to about two feet off the ground, but even when he pushed down on the handlebars, the bike kept flying up. He'd look down and push down at the same time, but every time he almost lost control of the bike. He couldn't remember this happening before, and it began to worry him.

"Alex," one of the boys called. "I'm not racing you. Not when you're riding that bike. It isn't fair!"

Alex screeched to a stop beside the boy and said, "Really. You're not kidding."

He wasn't joking, either. The bike was so close to perfect, it outclassed any other. It would *not* be fair to race against ordinary GTs and P.K. Rippers on the Radical. Alex gave each of the kids there a turn riding the Radical around the track, but he never once let it out of his sight. He was watching it with pride and with wonder, and was thinking about saving it, just for days like these, and never taking it to a race event.

"My dad's going to make me one too," Robinson piped up. The big boys looked down at him. "And it's going to have fire that shoots out of the tires. Like Batman's car . . . And I'm not lying."

Alex said, "Sure, Robinson, sure."

The little boy's face got bright red when he saw that no one believed him, and he rode into the parking lot to hide his angry tears.

That was where he saw Rick and Stu ride up on their Red Lines. They were wearing their helmets too, and they sped up to Robinson, shooting dust all over the place.

"Your brother here?" they asked him.

"Why?" he replied.

"Just wondering . . . 'Bye."

And they sped over the crest of the hill into the track area. Robinson followed them. His face had long finger lines through the dirt, left from his tears. He looked suspicious, instead of mad, now. Rick and Stu were watching Alex practice; but he didn't see them. Instead he sped around the track, shouting out his own moves, as if he were an announcer:

"Porter goes over the whoop-de-dos with no hands, Ma, and flies around the berm like he was inventing a new machine! . . . He's a bird! He's a plane! He's Super-Rad!"

Then he stopped at the end of the track, while the other kids took turns following him on their own bikes. Rick and Stu moved over.

"Hey, Porter!" called Stu.

"Hey, Super-Rad, or was it Super-Rat?"

"Yeah, hey, Super-Rat." Stu laughed.

Alex studied their faces and realized they were not being friendly.

134

"Rick's grounded because of you and Speedy Gonzales," said Stu. "He can't do anything—for months."

Alex walked up the starting hill, pushing his bike with his hands squeezed tight on the grips.

"So why is he here then?" he called over his shoulder.

"Guess!" called Rick.

"Duckbill platter pusses," said Robinson under his breath. "Jerks don't know zip-doodley-squat."

They pushed past him.

"Want to race, Porter?" asked Stu. He had a small lead pipe sticking out of his belt.

"Sure. Why not?" Alex responded.

"Whoever loses admits he's a loser, okay?" said Rick.

"Fine with me," said Alex.

"We'll start at the starting gate and keep going," said Stu.

"To the finish line," Alex agreed. "Catch me if you can."

"You can't race worth a monkey shine," shouted Robinson, "not against the Radical."

He was surrounded, then, by Alex's friends. They all stood in a cluster, watching. They were quiet until one of them called out, "You guys better keep this fair!"

Stu and Rick stood on either side of Alex. And they all three shot forward at the same time. Alex was far in the lead by the time they had curved around the first berm, but then Stu pulled an object out of his pocket and hurled it ahead, at Alex. It was a rock, and it clanked off Alex's rear tire, causing him to swerve and fall sideways. Then

135

Stu and Rick moved in on him, each on separate sides, and they banged up against the Radical as soon as Alex was back on it. They whammed and bammed against his pedals, tires, feet, cursing at him.

"Hey, leave him alone!" the boys were shouting at the edge of the track.

"That's not fair!"

"You're going to get in trouble!"

"I hate you, stupids!" came Robinson's voice, the loudest.

Alex pulled ahead again, when they came to the top of the last jump, and he sped along, flying over the whoop-de-dos, with his face blazing and his eyes burning and his hands pushing down hard on the handlebars. His shins were cut and bleeding, and he could see two dents and several scratches on the bike. He almost lost control of the handlebars and swerved when he looked at the ground. He heard them behind him, shouting, and felt the bike pull up, no matter how hard he pushed down, with his head and shoulders forcing down too.

"Keep moving, loser! Don't stop at the finish line!"

He did what they said and didn't stop. But as he rode by the crowd of his friends, he heard them call, "Here's Rennie!"

"Whew! Where?"

"In the parking lot!"

Then he pedaled faster, holding in his mind the image of Robinson, crying. He zoomed toward the parking lot. Rick and Stu were following as fast as they could, and another rock came flying at Alex. But this one bounced off his helmet. The bike jerked upward, swerved, but he got it back on target again.

A voice called: "Go for the road! I'll follow!" And he saw Rennie, on his bike too, racing out of the lot toward the foothill road. It was narrow and paved with tar. Waves of heat jiggled ahead of him like water, and the foothills rose up like a wall on his left. His mind was racing as fast as the bike. He heard Rennie's voice behind him calling, "Keep riding, Alex," and he knew he could keep the lead he had. However, it could only go on and on like this until one of them got tired, or a rock hit his wheel again and he would fall.

Wavering, he looked back once, down the long empty road, and didn't see anyone coming. He stopped and listened to the silence. Ahead of him was a road leading up La Caputa. There, towering above, was the monk's hood; his nose and his eyes, at this hour, were half open. His sagebrush nose was sticking out, a rocky ledge. Alex took a deep breath and slowly moved back the way he had come, listening.

The heat seemed to embrace his whole body and suffocate his breathing. His hands were wet with sweat on the grips, even inside his gloves. Then he saw them—around a bend. They were going for Rennie, and their faces were red with anger. Alex rode toward them. Rick and Rennie were squared off to fight, there by the edge of the road. Stu was moving back, and letting them fight it alone.

"Don't get in the way," he warned Alex. "Let them duke it out alone."

Alex looked at Rennie's round brown face; he had never seen it so far away from laughter before. His fists were raised, and he was advancing toward Rick.

Rick was stripped to the waist, his back burned red and sweaty. He had Stu's lead pipe in his hand, and it was raised to land a blow on Rennie.

"That's not fair!" Alex shouted. "You can't use that!"

"He can't? Why not?" asked Stu with a smile.

Rick started saying things to Rennie, about himself and Addie, and about how she had been really close to him; he made every word he said about her sound dirty. But when he started talking about his uncle, Alex listened sharply.

"My uncle made me apologize to you. . . . But you know what? It was him who made me take the bike, and it was him who kept it there at the house. He laid it all on me. And you know why I let him?"

Rennie shook his head, No.

"Because I thought it would really burn you to lose that bike. That's why. I thought it was yours, Chico."

"Shows you're really dumb," said Rennie.

"Why did your uncle want my bike?" Alex called out, trying to distract Rick from Rennie.

"You kidding? That bike could make someone very rich," said Stu. "Now shut up, Alex, or I'll start after you again."

Then Alex saw Robinson running up the road, by himself, and he realized his mother would kill him for letting his brother stay alone at the track.

"Damn . . . Here comes my brother," he muttered to

138

Stu. "I gotta tell him to sit down and shut his mouth."

Alex laid the Radical down by the side of the road and started walking toward Robinson. But as he passed Rick, he leaped out and grabbed hold of the lead pipe. He yanked it hard, so unexpectedly that Rick let it go and Alex backed away from them, with the pipe up, saying, "Okay, loser. Now fight fair."

And that's when the scuffle began: Rennie and Rick going at it with their fists, knees and heads, rolling in the dust. Stu was shouting angry words, first at Rennie, then at Alex. Alex was shouting encouragement at Rennie and curses at Stu. And Robinson was crying. Stu obviously wanted to get in on the fight; he kept jumping around, screaming instructions at Rick. But Alex kept the pipe in the air, directed at him the whole time.

The fight lasted about five minutes. It seemed like fifty. Rick and Rennie ended up bloody, with split lips and bruised backs. But Rennie was on top of Rick when Rick called it off, saying, "Okay, okay," several times.

Stu, in a rage, picked up the Radical and heaved it far off into the rocks and dust by the edge of the road. Then he mounted his bike and rode away without Rick.

Alex wiped the tears off Robinson's cheeks, though he couldn't stop him from making little sobbing sounds while his shoulders shook. But finally Rennie stopped him by picking him up and placing him on his bicycle seat.

"Calm down, Rob," he said, "I'm fine. I'll give you a ride back, okay?" he said, with blood all over his upper lip and nose.

Then Rennie and Alex turned to look at Rick, who was

bent over, as if in pain, but was pushing his bike forward.

"Maybe you'll be glad to know your uncle's going to get fried," said Rennie. And he went on, muttering in Spanish, under his breath.

Alex pulled the Radical out of the dust and examined the scratches made by its fall. He was mad, but he figured he could still ride it in the big race in Laguna. He test-rode it a short while, then waited for Rennie to catch up. While he was standing there, Addie Sparks shot by him on her bike, like a bolt of lightning, her red hair flying. He knew where she was going. It made him smile. Somehow he just knew that the next time he saw Rennie his face would be clean, almost as if nothing had happened.

While the boys were fighting on that dusty road, Rick's uncle was taken to the station by the police. Mr. and Mrs. Porter followed in their car, and spent the day making sure the sponsor was given a court date. They also called his manager at Rainbow Toys, telling her what had happened. And finally Mariel stopped the big beefy man on the steps of the police station and told him what she thought of him.

"If I ever see your face again, at any race track this side of the Mississippi, I'll publicly, over the speaker, let everyone know what a creep you are," she shouted. Her husband looked away, as if he didn't know her. "I can't believe any human being could do what you did. You come crashing in on a family sport and try to turn it into your own private playground. You abuse the trust of children, you use your own nephew—and all to make a few bucks! What did you do with our bike? Tell me that? Did you sell the design? Huh?"

The sponsor moved by her, smiling serenely, as if she was no more than a little gnat buzzing on his alligator shirt.

"Answer me, you big dummy!" she screamed and grabbed hold of his arm.

This time he turned around, still smiling, and said, "As if I would tell you anything. I guess you'll just have to wait and see, as far as your bike's design goes."

Then he pushed her hand off, and turned to find Mr. Porter staring him square in the face.

"If you won't have the manners to respond to my wife, then I won't have the manners to let this case stop in small-claims court. You're in big trouble—" and he hesitated, smiled, and said: "Pig."

The sponsor passed and climbed into his van, while the Porters stood watching.

"Want to come to the race Saturday, with me and the kids?" Mariel asked her husband, as she locked her arm in his.

"No, thanks," he said, his smile broadening. "I think I'll just stay home and play the violin."

"I can't say I blame you. The bike business is beginning to get wearing."

"Well, let's go pick up the kids at the track. I'm sure they'll be glad to hear that he's going to court. They'll know that adults can't get away with every rotten deed . . . right?"

"Right," she said. "They're such good kids. They never fight, or get in trouble."

They drove to the track, where Robinson and Alex were waiting, with big innocent smiles, as if nothing special had happened.

11

In Laguna the following Saturday the track was teeming with color and activity under a flat blue sky. The races were scheduled to last all weekend. People camped out overnight, some stayed at a nearby motel. Loads of prizes were displayed beside the trophies. The Pro Purse was to be $5000. Most of the best racers in the country were there, and several of them were scheduled to travel abroad for races too.

"Wow, Alex! You could go to France, Germany, Japan!" cried Mariel, "if you just had an honest-to-goodness decent sponsor."

It was noon on the second day and the family had found

a spot of shade to sit in while they ate their lunch. Alex kept the Radical right beside him all the time. He was coming in second in all his races, and felt discouraged.

"I don't think I'll ever get a sponsor, Mom, the way I'm racing these days. The bike wants to fly, or something. I can't get it to go over the jumps right."

"That's right. Blame it on the bike," she said, and snatched some potato chips out of his bag when he wasn't looking.

"Seriously. There's something weird about this bike," he said, and hung onto its handlebars as some boys came over to examine it and ask where he got it. He was glad he could now tell the truth about its make.

"My dad is an inventor," he told anyone who asked. "You'll see. This model will be famous someday."

No one doubted him, the bike was so swift and so pretty to look at. Now a short man stepped out of the crowd to look at the Radical, too. It was a man Alex had seen before. He was dressed in jeans, sneakers, and a polo shirt, and he looked very comfortable around the track. He squatted down until he was eye-level with Alex and the bike, and he ran his hands over the shiny frame. He had a sharp-featured face with bright blue eyes, and a surprisingly warm smile.

"This is a beautiful piece of equipment," he remarked. "You're Alex Porter, right?"

Alex nodded and glanced at his mother who was off in a trance, listening to music with Rosie's Walkman plugged into her ears.

"My name's Hal—Hal Taylor. I'm a factory sponsor— R. J. Products. You know our stuff?"

144

"Sure. I used to get it for my old GT," said Alex, and smiled, remembering this man from the bike store.

"Right. We manufacture seatposts, cranksets, grips, pedals—the works . . . How do you like this track? 1200 feet and plenty of room for passing. I think it's beautiful. Can't understand why you're not coming in number one on this trophy-catcher. What's the problem?"

Alex felt his face turn hot. "I don't know. Maybe I'm just not used enough to this bike."

"Listen. You could still get a first today. I checked. You could get the State Championship. You're a fine rider. You've got one more moto until the main, right?"

Alex nodded.

"I'm going to keep my eye on you and see if I can give you some tips. Okay?"

Alex nodded again.

"Oh yes . . . There's a practice area no one seems to know about—over beyond that playing field there. You might want to take some turns." He stood up then, rubbing his kneecaps, as if he had arthritis. "I'd like to sponsor you, Alex . . . That's what I'm getting at. Talk to you later."

And he walked away. Only eight riders could make it into the main, and all twelve, at this point, were pretty evenly matched in Alex's moto. He stood up, holding onto his bike. He wondered why, ever since he had the bike back, it caused him so much trouble. He figured he could win every time on his old GT, and almost wished he had brought it to the race instead of the Radical. Nothing on the bike had changed; he knew that. His father had examined it. Still, Alex felt almost superstitious about the way it wasn't working right. He wondered if the Rainbow man had put some kind of a curse on the bike.

"No, that's stupid," he said out loud.

"What is?" asked Robinson.

"You is," said Alex, and laughed, adding: "No. Just kidding. Come on. Let's go watch the races."

"Alex," said Robinson, "if you ever get a real sponsor, will we ever be at the same races again?"

"Sure, we will."

"But then I'll have to ask you for your autograph."

"Now you really are being stupid," said Alex.

Robinson's lower lip slipped out to sho how offended he was by Alex's criticism, but Alex didn't notice.

"Here come the 12-Experts for the final run to the main!" the announcer shouted. "Always a crowd pleaser, this moto is up at the gate and ready to go for the final . . . Yep. There they go, with Shelby Brown taking the lead. It's heavy-duty time! Paul Kendall is on Shelby's tail, but look at that—Paul thought it was lightning struck him—just Alex Porter on that dynamite bolt of speed, called the Radical, going over the double whoops, passing by Paul and tailing Shelby . . . Looks like he's aiming to be, once again, number two, with Shelby holding the lead this time, instead of Peterson in fourth . . . Alex wants to hex hit, but can't quite make it. He stays in second over the last whoops, so it's Shelby number one, and Paul and Peterson are neck and neck behind Alex . . ."

Alex ripped off his helmet; his hands were slippery and his face dripped dust and sweat. He shook his head at his

146

mother, angry at his number-two position—again.

"You still could take the main trophy, Alex," a man's voice said. It was Hal Taylor again. "The other guys have been doing third and fourth places all day. You can still win. Believe me."

"But the bike is doing something wrong, every time," Alex sighed.

His mother joined them then, her forehead creased and perplexed. Alex introduced her to the sponsor, and his mind drifted as the two of them talked BMX. He remembered the way he held the grips on the bike. He had to squeeze incredibly hard because the whole bike seemed to be tugging up from under him. It felt as if the front wheel was too lightweight for the rear. It seemed as if the bike actually wanted to fly, instead of following the laws of gravity.

"Come over here," said Hal, and nudged him out of his thoughts. "I want to show you something. Your mother agrees with me."

Alex followed him through the crowds of multicolored uniforms and spinning bicycle wheels to the playing field that bordered the track area and was a parking station for rows of campers.

"Let me give you a tip," said the man, and he took the bike out of Alex's grip. "See how you're holding on? Like this?"

Alex nodded.

"Well, when you go over the whoops and when you're at the top of the jump, don't panic and look down at the ground. That makes you push down. Let the front wheel

147

go up, the way it wants to. Understand? You're a big boy now. Don't look down when you're up."

Alex studied Hal Taylor's face, his blue eyes that were bright and honest like his father's, and he said, "Hey, thanks for telling me that. It sounds right!"

"No problem. Just keep saying to yourself, Don't look down when you're up, and you'll do fine."

"Wow, I hope so."

"Talk to you later," the man said, and he waved to a bunch of kids wearing uniforms from his factory. Alex looked at them closely. They ranged in age from ten to almost twenty, and he recognized some from the race where he saw Hal before. They were decent racers, but nothing for him to feel inferior over. They came in all shapes and colors, and were all native Californians. He imagined himself traveling with them, in a camper, probably, with sleeping bags and tents. They'd drive up and down the coast, following the races, and maybe even cross into Nevada. After a while spent with one sponsor, a racer would often switch to another, one more national, or even international; and Alex could see himself in a couple of years doing that, too.

"What are you staring at?" Robinson asked him.

"Nothing."

"You never tell me anything."

"There's nothing to tell. Come watch me practice something, okay?"

Robinson willingly followed him across the long green field, away from the crowds, until they could barely hear the speaker or the music. Out of sight of everyone, they stopped beside an abandoned construction site Alex guessed to be the test spot that Hal mentioned.

"I want to try something new on the Radical," he told Robinson. "You just stand and watch and tell me how I do."

Robinson, leaning on his bike, stared out from inside the shade of his helmet as his big brother pedaled to the end of the site. He was aiming toward a huge dirt hill, the kind of dump pile he had first learned to ride on.

"Watch!" Alex shouted.

Then he pedaled hard and fast, burning rubber all the way to the peak of the hill. There he lifted up his head, looked at the sky and hesitated, before relaxing his hold on the grips. His heart was pounding. Why am I afraid? he wondered. It's just a bike! And now he felt the Radical hold its space, front wheel lifted, and slowly, gracefully, rise before losing momentum and gliding down for a soft landing. Then he pedaled forward, at top speed, and rounded the hill to do it again. He was grinning, as if he had won the biggest race of his life.

Robinson jumped up and down and called out, "It looked like you were about to fly, Alex, it really did!"

"And it felt like it, too," said Alex breathlessly.

"How did you do it?"

Alex started to say, "Never mind," but then he stopped riding, so the bike sent up dust, and he backed up to stand beside his little brother. "You really want to know?"

Robinson nodded.

"I just stopped being scared. I stopped thinking that this bike was bigger than me. That's all."

"You were scared?" Robinson asked with some amazement.

"Yes, but don't tell anyone. . . . It's a secret, between you and me. Okay? Promise?"

"I promise," said Robinson proudly.

And he didn't tell anyone the secret, not even when everyone was clapping and shouting, as Alex practically flew through the main race into first place. He didn't tell when his mother asked Alex, "How did you do it?" And he didn't even tell when the sponsor shook Alex's hand, welcoming him into his factory team, saying, "You're not afraid to try anything, are you?"

It was a secret that grew with him.

ABOUT THE AUTHOR

Fanny Howe is the author of several novels for young readers, as well as novels and poetry for adults. She is now teaching in the creative writing program at the Massachusetts Institute of Technology in Cambridge. She became interested in bicycle motocross when her son started racing, and she has accompanied him around the United States to tracks in Massachusetts, Connecticut, and California.

Ms. Howe lives in Brookline, Massachusetts, with her three children, Ann-Lucien, Danzy, and Maceo.